TIMMY FAILURE

NOW
LOOK
WHAT
MISTAKES
WERE
MADE

STEPHAN PASTIS

CANDLEWICK PRESS

THE MEMOIRS OF TIMMY FAILURE

Mistakes Were Made

Now Look What You've Done

We Meet Again

Sanitized for Your Protection

The Book You're Not Supposed to Have

The Cat Stole My Pants

TIMMY FAILURE

MISTAKES WERE MADE

To my uncle George Mavredakis.
Thank you for everything.

A Prologue That Story-wise Is Out of Order

It's harder to drive a polar bear into some-body's living room than you'd think. You need a living-room window that's big enough to fit a car. You need a car that's big enough to fit a polar bear. And you need a polar bear that's big enough to not point out your errors. Like the fact that you've driven into the wrong house. Which, when it comes to cars in living rooms, is bad.

I should back up.
(The story. Not the car.)

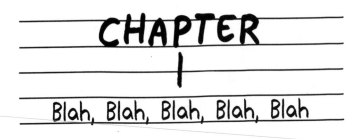

CHAPTER 1

Blah, Blah, Blah, Blah, Blah

All right, let's get the boring stuff out of the way. My name is Failure. Timmy Failure. I look like this:

Timmy Failure

Distinctive Scarf

My family name was once Fayleure. But somebody changed it. Now it is spelled as you see. I'd ask that you get your "failure" jokes out of the way now. I am anything but.

I am the founder, president, and CEO of the detective agency I have named for myself: Failure, Inc. Failure, Inc., is the best detective agency in the town, probably the state. Perhaps the nation.

The book you are holding is a historical record of my life as a detective. It has been rigorously fact-checked. All the drawings in here are by me. I tried to get my business partner to do the illustrations, but they were not good. For example, here is his depiction of me:

I have decided to publish this history because my expertise is invaluable to anyone who ever wanted to be a detective. Just read the reviews:

> "Invaluable to anyone
> who ever wanted to be
> a detective."
>   —Anonymous

But success did not come overnight for me. I had to overcome obstacles. Like these:

1. my mother
2. my school
3. my idiot best friend
4. my polar bear

And yes, I'm sure you have the same question everyone else does when I list these obstacles. Why am I best friends with an idiot? I'll get to it later. Oh, and I suppose I should say a word about the fifteen-hundred-pound polar bear.

His name is Total.

Total

Total's Arctic home is melting. So he wandered for food and found my cat dish. He is now 3,101 miles from his former home. Yes, that's a long way to roam for a cat dish, but we buy good cat food. Sadly my cat is now in Kitty Heaven (or perhaps the Kitty Badlands—he never was a friendly cat), but I still have the polar bear.

Initially Total displayed a fair degree of diligence and reliability, and thus I agreed to make him a partner in my agency. As it turned out, the diligence and reliability were a ruse. Something polar bears do. And I don't want to talk about it. I also don't want to discuss the change I agreed to make to the name of the agency, which now reads like this in our yellow pages ad:

TOTAL FAILURE, INC.

(WE WON'T FAIL, DESPITE WHAT THE NAME SAYS.)

And now I have to go. Because the Timmyline is ringing.

CHAPTER 2

The Candy Man Can't 'Cause He's Missing All His Chocolate

The call is from Gunnar. Classmate, neighbor, and now just another guy missing his Halloween candy. I get a lot of candy cases. They're not headline grabbing, but they pay cash money. So I wake up my partner and hop on the Failuremobile.

I should say a word about the Failuremobile. It's not actually called a Failuremobile.

It's called a Segway. And it belongs to my mother. She won it in a raffle. And she has set forth some restrictions on when and how I can use it.

I thought that was vague. So I use it. So far, she hasn't objected. Mostly because she doesn't know.

That touches upon one of the founding principles of Total Failure, Inc., which I've memorialized in ink on the sole of my left shoe.

The only complaint I have about the Failuremobile is its speed. If I ride it somewhere while Total walks, Total gets there first. That wouldn't be so bad if it weren't for the fact that in between, Total naps.

PUTT PUTT PUTT

So it isn't any surprise to me that when I get to Gunnar's house, Total is already there, doing something that he frequently does when he beats me to a house. Before I tell you what that is, let me just say this: first impressions are critical in the detective world. A client has to know at first glance that their detective is (a) professional, (b) classy, and (c) discreet.

All of this is undermined when the client's first impression of their detective is this:

CHOMP CHOMP CHOMP

I've lectured Total so many times on eating garbage from clients' trash cans that I now believe he is purposely sabotaging the agency. Fortunately for me, by the time I knock on Gunnar's door, Total has finished eating everything edible from the trash cans and is able to stand next to me on the porch.

Gunnar answers the door and escorts us to the scene of the crime. He points to an empty table by his bed. "My plastic pumpkin filled with candy was right there," he says while pointing at the tabletop. "Now it's gone."

I look at the tabletop. I can tell from the empty space that it is gone.

He starts listing the candy he had in the pumpkin. "Two Mars bars, a Twix, seven 3 Musketeers, five Kit Kats, eleven Almond Joys, five Snickers, an Abba-Zaba, and eight Hershey's Kisses."

Gunnar looks up at me. "You getting all this down?"

"'Course I'm getting it down."

"Let's start with the basics," I tell the client, "like payment. I take cash, checks, and credit cards." I don't actually take credit cards, but it sounds professional, so I say it.

"How much will it cost?" asks the client.

"Four dollars a day, plus expenses."

"Expenses?" asks Gunnar.

"Chicken nuggets for the big man," I say, pointing up at Total. Total roars, which looks intimidating until he falls backward and crushes Gunnar's desk.

That, I know, will be coming out of his chicken nuggets. I tell Gunnar that I anticipate a six-week investigation. Lot of witnesses. Maybe some air travel.

"I'll show myself out," I tell him.

As I walk down the hall, I pass his brother Gabe's room. Gabe is sitting on his bed, surrounded by candy wrappers. There is chocolate smeared all over his face and an empty plastic pumpkin on the floor.

Always on the lookout for clues, I make an important note in my detective log.

CHAPTER
3

The Timmy Empire Strikes Back

All I need to solve the Gunnar case is five minutes of peace. But I can't get it. Because of this man.

He is Old Man Crocus. He is my teacher.

And he stands at his beloved whiteboard for six hours a day to tell me things that could bore the fur off a squirrel.

Furless Squirrel

Old Man Crocus is 187 years old. He smells. And he is bent over like he's got a sack of potatoes hanging from his forehead.

Sack of Potatoes

That would be useful if I were making French fries. But I'm not. I'm building a detective agency empire. And there is nothing in my classroom that is going to help me get there. Except maybe the world map on the wall. Which is why I've taken it and filled in all the territories that will have Total Failure offices within five years.

A good teacher would reward that sort of initiative. But not Old Man Crocus. He says,

"What has Captain Thickhead done now?" and eliminates my hard work with correction fluid.

So I take my face and eliminate his.

I think that's tit for tat, but he sees it differently. So he moves me to a grouping of desks with the three "smart" kids in the hope that they'll rub off on me. They're surely hoping that *I* rub off on *them*.

One of them is Molly Moskins. She is a nuisance. She smiles too much. And she smells like a tangerine.

Molly
Moskins
(aka
Tangerine
Girl)

The rotund boy is Rollo Tookus. We have plenty of time, so we can talk about him later.

stanfurd

And the girl whose face I've obscured is someone I am never ever, ever, ever going to talk about ever, no matter what.

So fine, let's talk about the rotund boy.

CHAPTER 4

Meet Rollo Tookus

The first thing you need to know about Charles "Rollo" Tookus is that he is not smart. Yes, he has a 4.6 grade-point average, but that is only because he studies. Obsessively.

ROLLO
TOOKUS

If *I* studied, my GPA would also be 4.6, instead of what it currently is, which is .6 (if I round up). Why Rollo studies as Rollo studies is a mystery to everyone but Rollo.

If you ask him about it, he'll yammer on about how if he studies, he'll get good grades, and how if he gets good grades, he can one day get into a university called Stanfurd, and how if he gets into Stanfurd, he can get a good job and make lots of money. Detectives have a word for that.

BORING

In fact, that brings up another one of the founding principles of Failure, Inc., one which I've memorialized on the sole of my *right* shoe.

I'd feel sorry for the poor kid if he had a parent *making* him do all this, but he doesn't.

He *chooses* to do it. Which proves he's not smart. So the best I can do is to be supportive. Try not to criticize his deficiencies. Which can be hard when I hang out in his room and kick my feet up.

Unwinding in Rollo's room at the end of a long day at the agency is one of the ways I support him. I tell him about the cases I'm working on, and he studies. I think it's exciting for him to hear my stories. After all, it's obvious that Rollo would be a detective if he could. He just doesn't have the tools. That of course doesn't stop him from making amateurish comments about my cases, which can get very annoying.

Like today. I mentioned the Gunnar case and how he has a messy brother named Gabe, and Rollo said perhaps the stupidest thing he's ever said about one of my cases. Which was this:

"Maybe Gabe ate the candy."

Told you he was an idiot.

CHAPTER
5
Problems at the Office

Day Two on the Gunnar case. No leads. Office tense. Total and I know that the best thing to do in these situations is to give each other some space. Which is hard given that our office is my mother's closet.

Corporate Headquarters

The office wouldn't be nearly as cramped if my mother would get rid of all her clothes. I scheduled a teleconference with her over dinner last week to discuss it. Here's how it went:

That's how it is in business sometimes. You try to compromise, but other parties make it difficult.

I think it's because she's stressed. I'm not sure about what. I just know it must be something, because after our teleconference that night, she took her Segway for a ride around the block. That's her way of relaxing.

"This thing is a lifesaver," she said one time as she scooted past me. "I don't know what I'd do without it."

And that, my friends, is why I don't tell her it doubles as the Failuremobile.

But right now I have a business to conduct. And my cramped office conditions must be alleviated. So I've asked Total to look into a possible lawsuit against my mother. I've even given him some law books. So far all he's done is this:

While the space issue is a nuisance, it is actually only temporary. That's because I have my eye on the top floor of a new high-rise downtown. It has a view of the whole city.

According to an ad in the newspaper, the rent is $54,000 a month. That's steep, but if the Gunnar case goes well, it'll be a drop in the bucket.

That's the way the detective business is. You crack a big case. Word spreads. Bingo bango, you're making billions. But until then, the agency will have to get its work done amid my mother's clothes. And to be fair, the rent *is* reasonable (currently $0.00), and the only restriction upon us is my mother's rule that we cannot touch her clothes.

Which shouldn't be a problem.

For me, anyway.

CHAPTER 6

It Ain't Me, Gabe

With the Gunnar investigation stalled, I do something to humor Rollo Tookus. I take a statement from Gabe, aka the Slob. "Where were you on the night your brother's candy disappeared?"

"I was in my bedroom."

"Doing what?" I ask.

"Eating," he says.

"What were you eating?" I ask.

"Candy," he says.

That's when it hits me. The import of what he is saying.

So I make a note of it in my detective log.

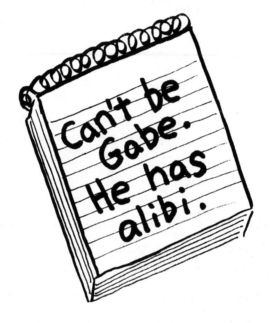

CHAPTER 7

Sad-Eyed Lady of the Lunch Recess

Lunch recess is the only opportunity I have to do global strategy planning for the agency. So I eat on a bench by myself. It is the only way I can ensure that the other kids don't see my work and commit an act of industrial espionage.

It is pitiful, though. Pitiful that as I sit there and concentrate, my business partner groans and moans behind a chain-link fence.

The school won't let him in. So he has to stand there until I finish the school day and walk him home. He doesn't talk about it much, but I know he finds it discriminatory. To protest the school's actions, I sometimes put a sign on him.

When lunch is over, we have fifteen minutes to play whatever we want. Most kids play kickball. I sit by the fence and pet Total.

And don't ask me about the girl whose face I've obscured in the illustration. She's the same girl as before, and I still don't want to talk about her. What I will talk about is the fact that my sitting by the fence is hard on the other schoolchildren.

Hard because I am popular and they want to spend time with me. But they can't because they are wary of my Arctic business partner. Which is prudent. Polar bears are fierce and unpredictable. Plus they are always on the lookout for seals, which a schoolchild bundled up for winter can resemble.

Which is which?

The only person who is not afraid of Total is the yard lady, Dondi Sweetwater. She's a nice enough woman. But she talks quite a bit. Plus she has absolutely no concept of the time pressures I am under due to the agency.

Total, on the other hand, can't say enough good things about her. That's because she's always giving me Rice Krispies Treats to pass on to him.

Total goes bonkers for those things. And that's a real problem. Because one day we could be captured and interrogated for trade secrets and someone could offer him a Rice Krispies Treat and who knows what that fat bear would do.

For that reason, I have asked Dondi to never share this vulnerability with anyone outside the agency. I've also asked her to never even say the words *Rice Krispies Treats* aloud but to refer to said items as "the goods." She has agreed to all my stipulations and, at my request, has put her assent in writing.

TOTAL'S FONDNESS FOR "THE GOODS" IS CLASSIFIED AND SHALL REMAIN SO. SO SWEARS Dondi The Yard Lady

I had to make her put it in writing because that poor woman really does like to talk. Especially to me. Which is why we spend most recesses together. But that's okay.

It's all part of being popular.

CHAPTER 8

Once Upon an Iceberg

At home that night, my detective's intuition tells me something is wrong. I've seen my mother pass in front of the house eight times on her Segway.

The previous record was six. So I know it is serious.

That night, I tell her she doesn't have to read to me in bed like she normally does. But she wants to do it anyway. She's a trouper that way.

Now, if I had my preference, I'd have her read me trade journals every night so I could keep up on the latest developments in detective technology. But someone big and furry says it's boring.

My business partner prefers a very particular type of story, one that is hard to find in most commercial bookstores. So to humor him, I am forced to handwrite the stories myself and give them to my mother to read. I even have to illustrate them. Here's how they all start:

And they all have to end the same way too, or he gets very upset and can't sleep soundly.

When she's done reading, my mom turns out the light and kisses me on the nose. I pull the blanket up to my chin and sneak a look at my business partner.

He liked the story.

CHAPTER 9

Sumo Interlude

I am up bright and early the next morning. And I am hiding behind a tree wearing a sumo suit.

I am waiting for a four-foot-tall female whose name shall not be uttered. When she passes, I am going to crash into her. With any luck, I will roll her into the curb.

It's not personal.
It's business. And I don't want to go into it.

CHAPTER 10

More Office Problems

I ask my business partner to do one thing while I'm out. Answer the phones. And there he is, wrapped in phone cord, with the end of the line ripped out of the wall.

It's days like this that make me question his commitment. As if that's not enough, there's a note from my mom on the office door. I know she senses the agency's rising fortunes, so I assume it's a job application. But it's not.

School called.
Said you called
in sick.
__NOT__
acceptable !!

That's the thing about my mother. She'd rather I waste an entire day at school than spend the afternoon doing sumo surveillance. I don't think she means to be misguided. I think it's the stress. She works full-time at a stationery store. And it doesn't pay super-well, so she worries a lot. I suspect that has something to do with what's been wrong with her lately.

Fortunately for her, she gave birth to a genius. A genius who will one day save the entire Failure clan (me, her, and even the polar bear, though he does not deserve salvation).

But for me to do my thing and create a multibillion-dollar detective agency, I need her to do one thing: fend off all time-wasting distractions.

By that I mean school. And on that count, she is failing.

I've asked her for a teleconference to discuss this and other things, but she is constantly rescheduling. I'm not pushing the issue for now, but I expect it will come up at her year-end review. That's the annual meeting where I sum up her strengths and weaknesses as a mother.

The way she is pushing this whole school thing is definitely going to hurt her review. But it won't be the worst review I give out this year.

That will be to this guy:

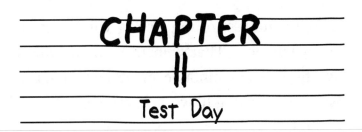

CHAPTER II

Test Day

It is test day. Multiple choice. So each of us has been given a stupid Scantron form where we fill in the bubbles to indicate our answers, A through E. I am going to use the bubbles to make a picture. Last time it was mountains.

With the rest of the time, I will work on agency business. That's when Old Man Crocus says he has an announcement. "For today's test, you are going to work in groups."

Rollo Tookus's eyes widen.

"Each group will turn in one test and get one grade."

Rollo gasps.

"The group you are seated with will be your group."

Rollo takes one look at me. And passes out.

I take no notice of Rollo. For I am focused on having to join forces with the One Whose Name Shall Not Be Uttered. So I express my opinion respectfully.

Rollo moans from the floor. Old Man Crocus shouts for me to get off the desk. Molly Moskins claps. It is something she does each time she gets to work with me.

Molly's clapping sends waves of tangerine smell everywhere. Soon we all smell like tangerine people.

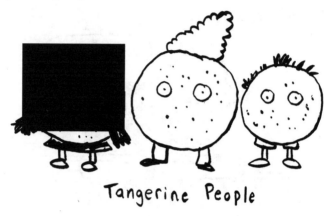

Tangerine People

Old Man Crocus shuts his eyes in frustration. He grits his worn wooden teeth.

He is one unhappy tangerine.

CHAPTER 12

Why Fuzzy-Wuzzy Wasn't

The one thing about the detective business is that it doesn't stop for you to solve the cases you've already got, like that of Gunnar's mysterious candy.

You just have to keep going. You can't crawl into some corner and give up.

Which is exactly what Max Hodges's hamster appears to have done.

"I found him like this when I got up this morning," Max tells me as I stand in his bedroom. "So I called you to see if you can figure out how he died."

Together we stare at the motionless hamster in the hamster cage.

"How do you know he's not alive?" I ask.

"Well," he says, handing me a photo, "because when he's alive, he looks like this."

Which is different than how he looks now.

So I ask Max the obvious. The stuff even an amateur detective knows to ask in a dead hamster case. "Did he have any enemies?"

Max says no.

"Did he have a lot of money?"

No.

"Was he depressed?"

No.

"Was he involved in criminal activity?"

No.

When it comes to crime, witnesses can clam up. So if you're a detective in these situations, you gotta put some of your own pressure on the witness. "Not involved in criminal activity," I say sarcastically. "Then what is this?" I point at a bit of hamster tube that appears to have a name scratched into it.

"I scratched my name on there," says Max.

"Looks like hamster graffiti to me," I say.

"It's not," he says.

So I grab the piece of hamster tube and put it in my pocket.

"Evidence," I say.

I show myself to the door, but when I go to open it, it won't budge. I duck low, expecting an ambush. That's when I see Total lying on the other side of it. His fat body is blocking the door.

I rap on the window with my fist until he moves, then walk to the curb to get on the Failuremobile.

The one my mother cherishes.

The one she said I can't use.

The one that isn't there.

I pause to jot a brief note in my detective log.

CHAPTER 13

The Small Business Community Is Under Siege

It's hard to focus on industrial sabotage when you're sitting at a parent-teacher conference. But this much I know. Somebody somewhere needed Total Failure, Inc., stopped. Our growing caseload was simply too much of a threat. So to stop us, they seized my mode of transportation.

The obvious move is to set up a security perimeter around the neighborhood and begin questioning witnesses. But I cannot. Because I am bookended by two amateurs who have never run a business.

To my left is my mother, who made me get in the car as soon as I got back from Max Hodges's house. To my right is Old Man Crocus. All I can think as he yaps is that the man has been teaching too long.

I say that because for the first time in his 150-year career, he faces the very real possibility that he will not advance all of his students to the next grade.

I suppose here would be a good place to tell you about the student who threatens that streak.

It's moments like this when I patiently wait for my mother to impress me with a spirited defense of her son. Maybe throw around some papers. Kick over a chair. Set fire to a desk.

Act of impressive mom

Instead, she nods.

For a woman who is one day going to be begging me for a job, she's doing a miserable job of impressing me.

So for now, I have to depend on my business partner, who I asked to do some reconnaissance in my absence. That means scoping out the scene of the crime and gathering information in a discreet way that does not draw attention.

It does not mean that which I found him doing when I returned home:

CHAPTER 14

Orange Juice. Shaken.
Not Stirred.

I am pacing Rollo Tookus's room like a man possessed. Because when you're a detective, you cannot be the victim of an unsolved crime. It is like a dentist with missing teeth. Or a gardener with dead flowers. And dead is what I will be if my mother finds out the Failure-mobile is gone.

So I hatch a plan to keep my mother from knowing. On paper, it looks like this:

But I can't focus. Because Rollo's head is rattling back and forth like a dashboard bobblehead. It is something that happens the night before every test.

He is especially nervous tonight because he did not do well on his last test. The group test. And that was because someone in the group made the Scantron form look like this.

I had to do it.

If Old Man Crocus was going to pair me with You-Know-Who, I had no choice but to throw myself upon the gears of the machinery and make the whole wretched process come to a halt.

Naturally Rollo didn't see it that way. His vision is too narrow. But not me. I see the big picture. And I know that sometimes you just have to take one for the team.

One day he'll thank me for that. But not tonight. Tonight the poor kid's head is shaking like the tail of an espresso-sipping rattlesnake.

Which reminds me.

One day I will think far enough ahead to tie one of the cartons of orange juice I drink from every morning to Rollo's head. It says, SHAKE WELL BEFORE POURING.

That would look like this:

And that is why I don't worry when I have a bad string of luck as a detective.

I know I could always be an inventor.

CHAPTER 15

Please Don't Squeeze the Detective

"Man's inhumanity to man
is a difficult thing to
behold."

—Timmy Failure

I still must get to work. So I have a new ride.
I call it the Totalmobile.

My business partner believes it is demeaning. I believe he's lucky to be employed.

I wrote *Greatness* on the side so that when people see us, they will know that we are great.

But that greatness did not prepare me for what I would see at the Weber residence.

For today it is the scene of total devastation. All marred by the remnants of someone inhumane. Someone determined. Someone whose weapon of choice comes in packs of six, twelve, and twenty. If you are squeamish, look away.

Toilet paper. It is everywhere.

And much of it hangs from the tops of trees, which tells me that these criminals were adept tree climbers. That's a major clue, and I make a note of it in my log.

I knock on the Webers' door. Jimmy Weber answers. He is in my grade.

"How's the family holding up?" I ask.

"Fine," Jimmy says. "It's not the first TP job we've ever seen."

"TP," I repeat to myself. I make another note in my log.

I ask Jimmy for a complete list of his enemies.

"Enemies?" he says. "I don't have any."

"Everyone has 'em," I tell him.

"No, really, I'm friends with everyone. People in my class. People on my soccer team. People that work with me on the school paper."

Bingo.

"I want a complete list of all the stories you've written," I tell him.

"Stories?" he asks.

"For the paper," I say.

"Oh, I don't really write stories. I just write what they're serving in the cafeteria this week. Why does that matter?"

I shake my head in disbelief. I try to remind myself that not everyone's a detective. "Listen, kid," I say. "Someone doesn't want that information out there."

"Who?" he asks.

I point to the hanging toilet paper.

"Someone who doesn't play games."

I go to hand him my card.

"Hey, Timmy, thanks, but I don't need your help anymore."

"What are you talking about?" I say. "You called the hotline."

"Yeah, over an hour ago. You took a while to show up."

It's true. I was late. Total fell asleep in front of my bedroom door, and I couldn't get out, which was very unprofessional on Total's part.

"Yeah, well I'm here now and I'm on the case," I tell him.

"Sorry," he says, "but I hired another detective. I hired—"

Don't say the name. Don't say the name. Don't say the name. Don't say the name. Don't say the name. Don't say the name. Don't say the name. Don't say the name.

"Corrina Corrina."

He says the name.

CHAPTER
16
The Chapter I Was Hoping to Put Off. The One About the Beast.

Some evil looks like Genghis Khan.

Some evil looks like Attila the Hun.

And some evil looks like this:

Corrina
Corrina

I really don't want to spend any more time writing about the Center of Evil in the Universe than I have to. First, because I spend absolutely no time thinking about her. And second, because I really, really hate her.

So let's be brief: The Beast owns a detective agency, the CCIA, which according to her, stands for "Corrina Corrina Intelligence Agency." I say it stands for "Corrina Corrina Is Asinine."

It is the worst detective agency in the town, probably the state. Perhaps the nation. Sadly, people are lured into hiring her by the look of her downtown office, which her rich, real-estate mogul father lets her use. It used to be a bank. It has pillars and a marble floor and a large safe. It looks like this:

As you can see, it's pathetic. And for those of us in the business, it screams, "Amateur." The stupidest, most unprofessional thing about it is that it is on the ground floor. That means that when I move into the top floor of my downtown high-rise, I will be able to throw things at her.

Making the situation even more ridiculous, the sad little girl has a huge stockpile of high-tech surveillance equipment, all furnished by her father. Cameras with zoom lenses, high-power binoculars, hidden microphones—you name it.

Now, maybe that seems impressive to you, but believe me, to someone skilled in the business, it says one thing:

SHe needs it.

Because real detectives do surveillance the old-fashioned way. With their own two eyes. And from all sorts of undesirable locales, such as laundry hampers. Which is a problem

when your mother needs to do the laundry a
day earlier than you expected.

CHAPTER
17

A Change Is Gonna Come

If you take one thing away from this chapter, let it be this: Timmy Failure does not lose a client to Corrina Corrina.

What she's done in taking the Weber file from me was unethical, illegal, and immoral. As a result, I have filed a complaint with the Better Detective Bureau. It is not the first such complaint I have filed against her. It is the 147th.

Because I do not own a computer or a type-writer, I have to handwrite the complaints on notebook paper. Here is one I filed last month:

Here is one I filed the week after:

I do not even know where Turkmenistan is. But it sounds far away.

Sometimes my complaints are more brief and to the point.

COMPLAINT

○ Corrina Corrina
○ smells bad.
○

And sometimes my complaints are of the follow-up variety.

COMPLAINT

○ YOU STILL have not dropped
○ Corrina Corrina over
○ Turkmenistan.

While these complaints are pending, I am also making two big changes to the agency. First, I bought a hat.

Please do not ask why it says BISCUITS. I do not know. Perhaps the prior owner sold biscuits. The point is that it makes me look more professional.

The second change is more substantive. I'm giving out free cheese.

So far, business is booming. At least for the free cheese.

Although everyone keeps asking me the same stupid question.

CHAPTER 18

Counting on My Accountant

I am sitting in my room. My mother made me.

I have two spelling tests tomorrow. And she wants me to study.

But I can't. Because of the Failuremobile.

Yesterday my mother said she was going to the garage to get it so she could take it for a spin around the block. I told her not to because there are spiders in the garage.

She told me she wasn't afraid of spiders.

I told her that I didn't mean to say *spiders*. I meant to say *giant anaconda*.

She dropped the topic and hasn't brought it up again. But I can't keep coming up with Amazonian reptiles. Eventually she is going to catch on. And before she does, I've got to get the Failuremobile. All of which means redoubling my prior efforts and putting significant resources into the search. Resources which Total Failure, Inc., may or may not have. So I grab the agency's accounting records for the last six months.

The records are one of the tasks I gave to Total when he came on board. I trusted him because (a) I did not have the time to do them myself and (b) he indicated to me that he had some accounting experience.

I thus expected that the books would accurately reflect Total Failure, Inc.'s gross revenue and expenditures for the fiscal year, all neatly added and subtracted in rows and columns. Like this:

But that is not what they look like. They look like this:

I search for my accountant.

I find him sitting on the heating vent.

Eating the free cheese.

I schedule a teleconference with my mother.

CHAPTER 19

The Answer, My Friend, Is Blowing on My Ear

"I need an administrative assistant," I tell my mother.

She is at the kitchen table. It is covered in bills.

"If you want me to study for school *and* run the agency, there's no other way."

She doesn't say anything, so I ask again.

"Listen. If you just float me the funds at a reasonable rate of interest, I can hire said administrative assistant."

She turns her head toward me. "Timmy, the stationery store cut back my hours. So right now I'm a little short of said funds."

I stare at the mess of paper on the kitchen table and pick up one of the credit card bills. In big bold letters, it says this:

TOTAL AMOUNT PAST DUE: $1485.23

"This is it?" I say, holding out the bill.

"This is what?" she asks.

"These sums," I say. "They're trifling."

I hold up the phone bill, the gas bill, and a doctor bill.

"With the amount of money Total Failure, Inc., will be taking in by the end of the fiscal year, I'll practically be able to pay this stuff out of petty cash."

She rests her cheek against the top of my head.

"It will be a loan, of course," I tell her. "Timmy Failure doesn't give handouts."

She wraps both her arms around my chest and squeezes me into hers.

"But when the agency expands, we'll most likely have a position for you, and we'll just deduct the funds owed from your paycheck."

She blows really hard into my ear. It's something she does sometimes because it makes me laugh.

"Be professional," I tell her.

She stops.

"Do it again," I say.

CHAPTER 20

Bean There, Done That

I am climbing Rollo Tookus's dresser to show him how the monkeys put the toilet paper in the Webers' tree.

He is barely paying attention.

"Sorry. Our English test is in four days. I can't focus."

So I tell him about Garbanzo Man.

"Who's Garbanzo Man?"

"He's the agency's new mascot. I built him out of old clothes and a paper bag, all of which I stuffed with newspapers." I show him a snapshot I keep in my pocket.

"What's the point?" asks Rollo.

"He's meant to convey a sense of fearsome greatness. I want to really intimidate the idiot that stole the Failuremobile. Intimidate the person so much that they give it back. I'm going to put him on our front lawn next to a big sign that says, GARBANZO MAN SEES ALL."

"That doesn't make any sense."

"You don't make any sense. You're not focused," I tell him. "Besides, you know nothing about marketing."

"Why'd you name him Garbanzo Man?"

"Because *garbanzo* means big."

"You're thinking of *giganto*. Garbanzo is a bean."

That's the thing about guys like Rollo Tookus. They think they know everything, but they don't.

"Anyhow, I have to study," Rollo says. "I've got my tutor coming over to help me in a half hour."

This is where I should tell you about the little fly in the ointment of my friendship with Rollo Tookus. Actually it's not a little fly. It's a garbanzo fly.

And it looks like this:

That's right. Rollo Tookus's tutor is none other than the Beast. And I don't want to rehash the umpteen arguments this has caused, so I'll just sum up our respective positions.

Rollo's Position: Corrina Corrina is really smart and helps him get A's.

Timmy's Position: Rollo is a big, stupid traitor.

Now, in fairness, I will say that when Rollo is around me, he tries not to say her name. He just says "tutor." And he gives me plenty of warning before she comes over, so I don't have to be in the same room with someone so unethical.

"All right, Rollo, I'm out of here. But do me a favor. Be on the lookout for clues. I think your tutor may have committed grand theft auto."

"What are you talking about?"

"I think she stole the Failuremobile."

Rollo closes his book and stares at me. "Her dad is rich, Timmy. I don't think she needs your Failuremobile."

"This isn't about what *she* needs, Rollo! It's what *I* need. And I need the Failuremobile. Don't you recognize industrial sabotage when you see it?"

"Listen, Timmy. I really have to study. If you're so sure she took it, why don't you pay a surprise visit to that bank where she has her office? See if it's there."

I have to admit it was the one decent tip Rollo's ever given me, so I drop a quarter in his pencil cup and pat him on the head.

I show myself out and walk down the gritty streets. Streets strewn with crumpled newspapers.

A whole lot of crumpled newspapers.

A trail of which leads to my front lawn.

And to the remnants of a man who was not as fearsome and garbanzo as I thought.

CHAPTER
21
You Can Always Go Downtown

I head downtown to do reconnaissance on CCIA headquarters. Because I am so well known and don't want to draw attention to myself, I go undercover.

Under my bed cover.

Even so, I hate to miss an opportunity to promote, so I use the back of the blanket.

Unfortunately the disguise does not help. And I am hounded by admirers.

But I do not mind. For on these downtown streets, I sense it.

The whole world has changed.

Changed because in the shadow of the future home of Total Failure, Inc., I see my destiny.

A destiny with which no man can tinker.

I am the soon-to-be head of the world's largest detective agency.

A multibillion-dollar employer of thousands who made it big by adhering to one simple credo: Greatness.

I am a detective without peer.

A visionary without limits.

A pioneer of tomorrow whose only challenge now is to remain humble.

So for now, I walk humbly down the sidewalk to the pathetic bank that is CCIA's headquarters, all to follow up on Rollo's tip about the Failuremobile. A tip that will prove to be wrong. Because Rollo Tookus is always wrong.

But that is okay.

Because the tip has brought me here.

To the site of my skyscraper of greatness.

Which is right next door to the bank.

Behind which is something I recognize.

The whole world has changed.

CHAPTER 22

Happiness Is Not a Dumb Blanket

Here's how this chapter should have gone:

Timmy Failure runs to the back of the bank. He seizes the Failuremobile. The Evil One bursts out of the bank's front door. Timmy seizes her by the collar of her evil coat.

"I have caught you, Evil One."

The Evil One shrieks.

"Your shrieks will avail you not," Timmy declares, "for you have been caught red-handed."

The Evil One cries.

"Your tears will avail you not," Timmy declares, "for you are history. As is your agency. It is all over. You are through."

Head down, hands cuffed behind her evil back, the Evil One calls out to Timmy as she is escorted to the police van.

"What do you want, Evil One?" asks a gracious Timmy.

"To tell you one thing," she replies, drooling with envy from one corner of her sad little mouth.

"Say it," Timmy commands.

"You are greatness personified," she says.

But that is not how this chapter will go. Because before all that could happen, this did:

That's right. The United States government stopped me by snagging a corner of my bed cover on one of their mailboxes. Why?

A bribe.

By whom?

Her nickname rhymes with the Weevil Bun.

Let me just say this: It's a sad day when the government of the people, by the people, and for the people decides to affix those people to mailboxes.

But affix me they did.

And trapped I was.

Until twenty minutes later, when I realized I could take the blanket off my head.

Only to see I was too late.

For the Failuremobile was gone.

Surely whisked off by the same government officials who affixed me to the mailbox.

But okay. Now I knew the odds. Me against

the Weevil Bun and all the governments of the world. Daunting for most. But I am not most. I am Timmy Failure. And no person or government or force of nature can stop me.

Except maybe being cold at night because I forgot to retrieve my blanket and can't depend on a "friend" to share his.

CHAPTER 23

The Timmynator's Judgment Day

Surrounded by dingoes.

Buried alive.

Doing math.

$$4840 \div 16 = \underline{\hspace{2cm}}$$

These are just three of the horrific places I'd rather be than the place I currently am.

Which is standing next to the Furious Rage that is my mother in the garage.

"Where is it, Timmy?" she shouts. "Where is my Segway?"

"What are you doing out here?" I answer.

"Cleaning out the garage," she says. "And I want to know where that Segway is!"

"Why are you cleaning out the garage?"

"Timmy, tell me where that Segway is!"

My left eye twitches. Then my right. It is something that happens when I'm nervous.

"I don't know."

She says nothing.

I say nothing.

And it is then that I see the fury disappear from her eyes. Replaced by something worse. Something I cannot surmount.

Mom tears.

I shout out the first desperate thing that pops into my large brain. "Molly Moskins needed it for a play!"

This stuns my mother *and* me.

"Who's Molly Moskins?" she asks, wiping the corner of one eye.

"An annoying girl who smells like a tangerine," I want to say.

Tangerine

But I don't say that. I say this: "A girl in my class. She's putting on a school play. And the main character drives a Segway. Don't ask me. It's her lousy play."

My mother pauses, her frustration subsiding. "Well, you should have asked, because it wasn't yours to loan."

"I know," I tell her. "Mistakes were made."

"Well, when can she return it?"

"Next week," I blurt out, "when the play is over."

Stupid me. I should have said next month. Bought more time. Those mom tears have clouded my judgment.

"Fine. But it better be returned *that day.*"

I saunter out of the garage. Trying to avert suspicion. Give my mom a quick wave. Dumb move. I never wave. Get it together, man.

Once out of her sight, I run for it. I know that I have to get to Molly Moskins before she does. Get our stories straight.

Granted, my performance wasn't pretty. But it worked.

And at least it adhered to my brilliantly conceived plan concerning the missing Failuremobile.

CHAPTER 24

The Furry Burrito

I do not like Señor Burrito.

She is Molly Moskins's cat. And every time I turn my head, she dunks her paw into my tea.

"She likes you!" says Molly Moskins. "That's how she shows it!"

I am tolerating this because I need Molly Moskins. Need her to corroborate my lie. So I am on her porch, and we are having a tea party.

"We should have a tea party once a week! It would be wondermarvelously splendiferous!" shouts Molly, displaying her tendency to use words that do not exist. She has been so excited from the moment I showed up at her door that she has not stopped yapping. I have not even had the chance to tell her that her female cat is a Señora and not a Señor.

"Molly, we need to talk about something."

"Oh, I love to talk," she says, pointing at my hat. "Do you like biscuits?"

I turn to face her, staring directly into those bizarrely mismatched pupils.

Mismatched Pupils

"Molly Moskins, my agency needs you."

"Ooooh," she says. "A modeling agency? You probably want me for my eyes."

"No, Molly," I explain, "it's not a modeling agency. It's a *detective* agency."

As I say this, I hear a *sploosh*.

It is Señor Burrito.

And she has taken advantage of my head turn to dunk *two* paws into my tea.

"Molly, my agency solves major international crimes. It is on the verge of being a multibillion-dollar corporation. The largest of its kind."

I let that sink in. Her mismatched eyes widen. "I *love* biscuits!" she says, pointing at my hat again.

I stand up to leave. "You're wasting my resources, Molly. And I have cases to solve. I'll show myself out."

But before I can walk down the porch steps, she rushes to block my way. The sudden movement sends tangerine smell everywhere. "Don't leave!" shouts the Tangerine Girl. "I have cases! Lots of cases!"

She grabs my hand and runs inside toward her bedroom, where she slides open her closet door.

"My shoes are missing!"

Behind her is a large shoe organizer. It is filled with dozens of shoes.

"Well, not *all* of them are missing. But many of them. Someone international stole them!"

Finally. An international case.

I return to the porch table to take copious notes. The first of which is this:

Do not leave Señor Burrito unattended.

CHAPTER
25
No Jet for You

You cannot rent an F-16 fighter jet.

F-16

At least that's what they'll tell you if you and your polar bear walk into an army recruiting center. Nor will they give you a Chinook helicopter.

Chinook

I explain that I am only going to level a bank. Not even a classy one.

"I can give you this," the army recruiter says, pointing to the water cooler and handing me a Dixie cup.

 ← Dixie cup

Total licks his lips.

"Sir, it appears you don't understand," I tell him. "I've declared all-out war against the Evil One."

He looks up from his paperwork. I stare back at him. "She's a four-foot-tall menace to society."

He rubs his eyes. "Listen, son. I've got work to do. If you're interested in joining the army, come see me when you're eighteen."

What did I expect from the same government officials who affixed me to the mailbox?

God knows what the Evil One has told them about me. The lies, the defamatory statements.

Surely she has attempted to frame me as a loon.

Which is why I wore the shirt I wore to the recruiting center that day.

Sadly, my business partner took no such steps to ensure that he, too, made a good first impression. I tried to explain to him that this was the army. An army with rigorous weight requirements.

185 LBS.
Ideal

And that he didn't fit them.

1,500 LBS.

**One
big
fatty**

But no. The big guy refused to lose weight. So when we walked into the recruiting office to rent a fighter jet—*wham*—we made a sloppy first impression. Just like I told him we would.

I think when my all-out war with the Weevil Bun is over, I'll do the poor mammal a favor. Like send him to business school. Maybe there they'll teach him what a Dixie cup is.

And maybe the next time we walk into an army recruiting center, we won't get kicked out again for doing this:

CHAPTER 26

Late-Night Epiphanies of the Sole

I wake at three a.m.

With a revelation.

(These things happen to good detectives. Our large brains never stop.)

Normal brain

Timmy's brain

And that revelation was this:

When I was with Molly Moskins and told her I was going to leave her house because I was a very busy detective, she stopped me and asked me to stay, suddenly claiming that many of her shoes had been stolen. I asked her to identify one of the stolen shoes. She pointed to a red shoe in her closet and said the other one was missing.

But she was hiding it behind her back.

Missing Shoe

That's when it hits me. What she was up to. So I make a note of it in my detective log.

CHAPTER 27

Grabbing the Bull by the Horns

Something is wrong with our educational system.

I say that because it is boring.

If educators really wanted us to learn, they would include little things during the school day that would make learning more interesting.

For example, put Rollo Tookus and a bull in an enclosed space.

That would teach me to never play with bulls. Instead, Rollo Tookus is my study partner. And he's dull as sand.

The way this whole study partner thing works is that the teacher pairs you with someone else in the class. You teach the lesson to him. He teaches the lesson to you.

Today's lesson is about identifying conjunctions. Here's how Rollo teaches me.

Here's how I teach Rollo.

"Knock it off," Rollo says. "Crocus will see us."

"No, he won't," I tell him. "He's reading Key West brochures at his desk."

"What for?"

"Who knows? Listen. I need your help."

"With what?"

"You need to infiltrate the CCIA."

"Infiltrate what?" he asks.

Old Man Crocus raises the tips of his eyeglasses above his vacation brochures. "Do you two not have enough to do?"

"We do, Mr. Crocus," Rollo says. What a butt kisser.

I lower my voice. "It's Corrina Corrina's intelligence agency. She's got my Failure-mobile. I saw it there myself."

Story Refresher ➜

"Shhhh," Rollo says quietly. "I don't want anything to do with your stupid plans."

"Okay," I tell him. "That's fine."

"Good," he says.

"But I think the next test is another group test," I tell him. "Hope I can do as well as I did the last time."

Rollo's head starts to shake like a maraca.

← Maraca

"Fine!" he says. "I'll do it. Now are we done?"

So I add one more thing.

"How do you feel about bulls?"

CHAPTER 28

Home at Safe

"You look fine," I tell Rollo.

"I do not look fine. I look stupid."

He is dressed as a Shasta daisy.

"How is this supposed to get me into Corrina Corrina's bank?" he asks.

"We've gone over this."

"Say it again."

"You're Dickie the Daisy. You're part of the Human Flower Parade."

Artist's Rendering of what Human Flower Parade Might Look Like

"So why am I stopping at a bank?"

"Because Dickie the Daisy wants to open an account."

"But she's just gonna say it's no longer a bank. It's the CC-whatever."

"Doesn't matter. By that time, you're done looking around. Scoping the place out."

"Why don't I just go as myself?"

"Too suspicious. She knows we're friends."

I hand him four quarters. "What's this for?" he asks.

"Bus fare. You can't ride the Totalmobile. You'd blow your cover."

"I can't do this."

"You'll be fine."

But no. He would not be fine. He would be Rollo.

What follows next is so aggravating to my professional sensibilities that I hesitate to include it in this book. It demonstrates how even a brilliantly conceived plan such as this can be decimated by the bumblings of a moronic amateur. To distance myself from it, I have made Rollo write it in his own hand.

MY ACCOUNT

BY ROLLO TOOKUS

2:55 PM — ATTEMPTED TO BOARD BUS.

2:56 PM — BUS DRIVER YELLS, "HEY, WEIRDO, GET OFF MY BUS."

2:57 PM — BEGIN LONG WALK TO BANK.

2:59 PM — DAISY PETALS POKING PEOPLE IN EYE. PEOPLE MAD.

3:01 PM — ANGRY MAN WITH HURT <del>EAR</del> EYE
         STARTS PLUCKING OUT MY PETALS.

3:04 PM —

ME NOW
↓

4:30 PM — ARRIVE AT BANK.
       <del>RING G——</del> KNOCK ON DOOR.
       CORRINA CORRINA SAYS,
       "WHO ARE YOU?"
       I SAY — "DICKIE THE DAISY."
       SHE SAYS I LOOK LIKE A SAD BUNNY.
       I TELL HER, "I'M DICKIE THE
       SAD <del>DAISY</del> BUNNY." SHE SAYS,
       "WHAT THE HECK IS GOING ON HERE?"

4:31 PM — ~~STUFF~~ MY HEAD STARTS SHAKING.

    CORRINA CORRINA SAYS, "IS THAT

      YOU, ROLLO?"

    I SAY, "NO, CORRINA CORRINA."

    ~~xxxxxxxxxxxxxxxxxxxxxxxxxx~~

4:32 PM — COVER <u>BLOWN</u>

    CORRINA CORRINA SAYS,

    "COME INSIDE, ROLLO.

    TELL ME WHAT'S GOING ON."

    <u>TOTAL</u> <u>PANIC</u> NOW.

    I SAY, "BIG PARADE.

    ME DICKIE. DICKIE WANT

    OPEN BANK!"

4:34 PM — ~~Crom this offers you glass~~
~~water. I say~~

CORRINA CORRINA CONCERNED
FOR MY HEALTH. HEAD WON'T
STOP SHAKING.
  CORRINA CORRINA OFFERS ME
A GLASS OF WATER. I SAY,
  "WATER NO.
      ME NEED
      LEAVE!"
          CAN'T SPEAK.

CORRINA CORRINA RECEIVES
PHONE CALL. WALKS OUT OF ROOM.

I TRY TO DO ~~MISSION~~ MISSION.

CHECK OUT PLACE.

FIND GIANT ROOM

WHERE BANK KEEPS SAFE.

WALK INSIDE.

HEAR SOUND OF

GIANT STEEL DOOR

BEING CLOSED.

4:35 PM TO 8:30 AM:

<u>Locked in Safe</u>

I really don't want to go into all the stuff Rollo did during that long night:

- Hyperventilating when he phoned me on his little emergency cell phone
- Calling me unfortunate names
- Not saying thank you when I called his mom for him and lied, saying Rollo was spending the night at my house
- Not listening attentively as I read him my copyrighted work "Surviving Enemy Capture on Beans and a Smile"

- Scaring the poor janitor who came to clean the bank that morning, only to find a mutant bunny

The only regret I have from that night is the inadequate job Rollo did regarding reconnaissance. Because when I asked him for a blueprint of the bank, I expected more than this:

CHAPTER 29

Movin' On Up

So here's why my mom was cleaning out the garage:

We're moving.

She says that with all the stuff going on with her work, we have to move into an apartment.

All of this is neither here nor there because we will soon be making more money than is decent.

But the short-term effect is that Total Failure, Inc., will finally be freed from the degradingly small closet in which it is currently confined. And that can only boost workplace morale.

I've scheduled a teleconference with my mother to discuss the new office space I'll have in the apartment. I've even submitted a design schematic for how the apartment should be laid out.

In a further upswing of good fortune, I've solved the Weber case.

Perhaps you recall it. If not, look here.

I focused all of my resources on it in order to show the Weevil Bun that I am not a detective to be trifled with.

How did I solve it?

Clue No. 1: Jimmy Weber said it was not the first "TP" job his family had seen. *TP* stands for "tiny person." And who's a tiny person?

Besides, we already know Molly Moskins is an international shoe thief. That's called recidivism (i.e., a tendency to relapse into criminal behavior).

But the biggest clue of all was the second one. One that I stumbled upon quite accidentally.

You may recall that while at Molly Moskins's house, I drank a fair amount of tea (at least before Señor Burrito sat in it). As a result, I needed to use the facilities.

And that's where I saw it. Hanging for all to see.

That's right. Toilet paper. The weapon of choice for the Webers' attacker.

In the bathroom of Molly Moskins.

The girl's on one heck of a crime spree.

CHAPTER
30

The Chute Heard Round the World

Clang kong ding a bing ding dong.

Is not a new song.

It is the sound the trash makes as it falls down the chute in our new apartment building. I am familiar with it because it is directly adjacent to Total Failure's world headquarters.

In the hallway.

That's right. Ignoring my repeated requests for a teleconference, my mother rented a tiny one-bedroom apartment. Now I sleep on a fold-out couch in the den.

And my corporate headquarters is by the trash chute in the apartment building's hall-way.

Normally I'd call a board meeting to discuss this untenable arrangement. But I can't. Because I do not have the support of half the board.

That half is happier than ever.

CHAPTER 31

Ebb and Flo

Deep in the rat-infested bowels of the earth.

At the end of a maze of torchlit tunnels.

Guarded by attack dogs.

Is where the Failuremobile is.

I don't know that for sure. But it's my detective's instinct. Which is rarely wrong.

And those bowels are most likely located below CCIA headquarters. Although I can't yet confirm that either. Because someone was a bad daisy.

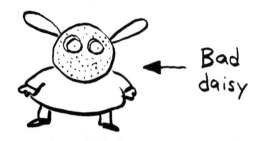

Bad daisy

Seizing the vehicle from the vicious dogs is a natural job for Total. He is the top of the Arctic food chain. But the last time I saw Total interact with a dog, he did this:

That's the problem with an Arctic predator like Total. You give him a seal and *wham*—he's

got lunch. But you give him a dog and *wham*—
he's got companionship.

To give Total better odds of seizing the Failuremobile, I've begun sending letters to the Weevil Bun. Letters containing subliminal messages.

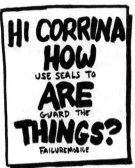

But for some reason, all the letters have come back stamped UNDELIVERABLE. Maybe it's how I'm addressing them.

Those aren't the only letters I'm having trouble delivering. Lately all my complaints to the Better Detective Bureau have also been getting kicked back to me. Like this one I filed after the Rollo bank incident:

I suspect from all this that the United States Postal Service is in the back pocket of the Weevil Bun. First they affix me to a mail-box. Now they block my mail.

Unable to rely on the postal service, I have decided to embrace technology.

The cost was higher than anticipated.

Thus, I scheduled a teleconference with my mother. Here are the minutes:

Fortunately I have options. Like my local library. And that is where Flo the Librarian comes in.

Meet Flo.

CHAPTER 32

Emily the Fist

You do not want to exceed the twenty-minute maximum for Internet use at my library. Because if you do, you see this:

That's an unhappy Flo. And *Flo* is not short for *Florence*. It's short for "Misshelve my books and the blood may FLOw."

I've never actually seen Flo the Librarian pummel anyone. But there've been rumors. Rumors of users wandering into the stacks and not returning. Fingers lost in card-catalog drawers.

So people do not misshelve books at my library. They do not tear pages out of magazines. And they do not ask stupid questions.

This arrangement works for me because Flo and I are professional colleagues. For example, he knows I have connections. Connections that if need be could one day spring him from the clink. The pokey. The big house.

The Big House

And I, in turn, know he's looking out for the Timmynator. For example, say I want to go over the twenty-minute time allotment for Internet usage. I just give him a look. And he gives me a grunt.

Professional Colleagues

Sure, it's a special privilege. Something not available to the common man. But that's the way the seamy underbelly of detective work is. Looks are traded. Bodies disappear.

Internet time limits are exceeded.

And Internet time is what I need right now. Because I'm building a website.

Well, *I'm* not. Flo is.

He saw me trying to do it myself and grunted. So I got up. And he sat down. And he started pounding on the keys with his big chubby fingers.

I told him I wanted the first screen to say this:

Then the second screen to say this:

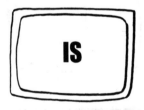

And the third screen to say this:

And the fourth screen to say this:

But Flo did something wrong. And now when you log on to the site, you see this:

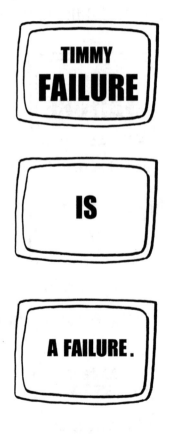

I'd say something to Flo about it, but I need to pick the right moment. And those are scarce. Scarce because when Flo sits behind his librarian's desk, he reads. And Flo does not like to be disturbed. Word is he reads books on how to kill things. And how to dispose of dead bodies. And how to crush things with your fist. I actually saw one of the books once. It had an odd title:

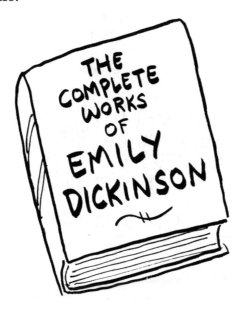

I'm assuming it's titled that because this Emily woman has written multiple books on crushing things with your fist. But then I looked her up on the Internet.

And if she can crush things with her fist, her photo is somewhat misleading.

EMILY DICKINSON
Crusher of Things with
Her Fist

CHAPTER 33

Milking Technology for All It's Worth

My World Wide Web site is not the only way I am changing the course of history. I am using the library's computers to send electronic mail. Or, as some in the detective industry like to term it, "e-mail."[1]

Electronic mail and World Wide Web sites are all part of my multipronged strategy to grow the business and destroy the Corrina. I obtained the Weevil Bun's electronic mail address from a flyer she posted in the library.

---

1. Do not attempt to memorize all these industry terms. They are highly technical. I have written the narrative in such a way that terms like this can be contextually understood by the average reader.

The flyer was defamatory.

The defamatory nature of the flyer is the subject of an electronic-mail complaint I have sent to the Better Detective Bureau.

To: BetterDetectiveBureau@geemails.com
From: TimmyFailure@yahoos.com
Subject: Defamation

I am inferior to no one.

I am also sending bogus electronic mails directly to the Weevil Bun herself. The purpose of these communications is to provide her with false leads. Waste her agency's resources. Send her on futile searches. Here is one I sent yesterday:

To: CorrinaCorrina@geemails.com

I am a cow that may have witnessed a murder.

Please find me so we can talk.

P.S. If it helps, I go, "Moooooo."

Too bad the library's scanner was not working.

Otherwise, I would have included this helpful map:

I am somewhere around here.

CHAPTER 34

Zero, My Hero

Some say the zero was invented by the Mayans. They say it was a big deal. I do not know why. But I do know that without it, you could not write this score:

That's our group English test. The one Rollo was worried about.

(Well, the most *recent* one he was worried about, anyway.)

But he was out sick. So that left just me,

Molly, and the Weevil Bun. And our teamwork was not ideal.

That left the Weevil Bun to answer all of the questions herself. So she did. And through dumb luck, she got them all right. But I could not share answers with a moral degenerate. So after she turned in the test, I grabbed it and changed all the answers. *A*'s became *B*'s. *B*'s became *C*'s. *C*'s became *D*'s.

And our A became an F.

That was too much for the Weevil Bun. So she complained. Said she no longer wanted to be in a group. And here's how Old Man Crocus responded.

The man is crumbling. I don't know what part of the educational system finally did him in, but I do have an educated guess.

That guess is about the only part of me that *is* educated right now. Because Crocus has given up. No more parent-teacher conferences. No more calling me Captain Thickhead. No more putting me with the smart kids. Now he just sits at his desk reading travel guides. Sometimes in a palm-tree shirt.

Palm-tree shirt

And when that <u>doesn't</u> work, he pulls out a little hula-girl statue and watches her hula.

Hula
Hula
Hula

He doesn't even seem to be bothered by the moral stand I took against the degenerate Weevil Bun on the latest group test. Though he does seem to resent one thing.

My fans.

Wasn't Timmy's Scantron amazingastic!

CHAPTER 35

Raisin Heck

When a bowler gets three strikes in a row, it is called a turkey. Here is another bowling turkey:

His name is Crispin Flavius. And here is everything I know about him:

1. He bowls.
2. He is dating my mother.
3. I call him "the bowling turkey."

I met him yesterday. He was sitting at my dinner table eating raisins. So I guess I know a fourth thing about him:

    4. He eats raisins.

I should say here that I loathe raisins. Though that did not stop me from initiating a friendly dialogue.

My mother said they met somewhere. And then she said something else. But I didn't hear any of it because it was then that I noticed the bowling turkey's upturned collar. So I tried to help.

Then I noticed something growing under his lower lip.

Then I noticed he only had one earring.

Disturbed by our exchange, I retreated to the bathroom to record an accurate assessment of him in my detective log.

When I returned to the dinner table, I was met with silence. I looked at my mother. "Crispin would like it if you'd take your hat off for dinner," she said.

"Gentlemen don't wear hats to dinner," he added.

I responded as best I could.

That was not received well. So my mother sent me to my room. But I don't have a room. I have a foldout couch.

So I took Total and went to Rollo's house. Where I was not received well either.

CHAPTER
36
Eureka

There's no point trying to explain a principled stand to Rollo. So the next time I see him, I bring him a gift.

To further lift his spirits, I bring up the Molly Moskins case. I don't really want his input. But it makes him feel good.

"I can't do this right now, Timmy. You've ruined my GPA."

"So you think I should arrest her?"

"I think I need to study."

"If I don't, no shoe is safe. And God knows what she'll do with toilet paper."

Rollo closes his book and turns to look at me. "If I tell you what I think is happening, will you let me study?"

I lock my hands behind my head and laugh. "Okay, big guy, shoot."

"Molly Moskins likes you. She wants you to spend time with her. So she hides her own shoes and pretends that they're stolen."

I laugh so hard I have trouble catching my breath.

"Sorry about that," I tell him. "It's just hard sometimes to listen to the musings of amateurs."

"Fine. I told you what I think. Now can you go? I have ten minutes before I have to go meet my tutor."

His
evil
tutor

"I thought the Weevil Bun came here," I say.

"It's not for tutoring. She left something last time she was here. I told her I'd return it."

"Then let me follow you. Knowing where she lives is vital intelligence."

"*I* don't even know where she lives," he says. "I'm meeting her at a coffee shop."

"You're a traitor and a fiend," I tell him. "So what did she leave?"

"Her backpack," he says.

I look at the backpack. It has an aura of badness.

Aura of badness

"You should burn it to cleanse the room," I tell him.

"I'm going to the bathroom," he says. "When I come back, can you please be gone?"

So he walks out.

Leaving me with the backpack.

I don't want to rifle through it. But it's obvious that Rollo's departure is a subtle signal for me to do just that.

So I do what he wants me to do and look through it.

And all I find are stupid schoolbooks and pencil cases and scarves (oh, trying to be like me?).

← Scarf

Until I get to the last pocket.
And find the Holy Grail.

CORRINA CORRINA'S DETECTIVE LOG

CHAPTER
37
Da Corrina Code

With no privacy to be had in my trash-chute office, I rush to the library with the enemy's secrets. I run in a crooked line to avoid assassins.

I enter the library. Nod to Flo. He clears a cubicle. I check for bombs.

I post Total at the rear entrance. Protection for my exposed flank.

Perimeter secured, I begin reading the log. Which, to demonstrate my fairness, I present to you here without comment.

Other than the comments I've written all over the attached sticky notes.

Monday, October 16

Tonight I sit in my room alone.
Dad still at work. Nanny watching T.V.
I go to bed before Dad gets home.

Tuesday, October 17

I wake up. Nanny says Dad
left early. Big box for me on the
breakfast table. Inside is a pair of
binoculars. Card says, "To help you
with your next case. Love, Dad."

↑ Likely story. Probably stealing

Dad right. ↗
You need help.

Thursday, October 19

Jimmy Weber offers me case.
I accept as favor to him.

Friday, October 20

I solve Weber case when I
overhear Chris Thompkins brag
he TP'ed the Webers.

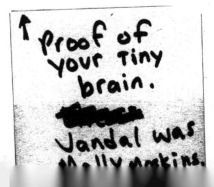

GROSS
distortion
of truth
FILE
STOLEN
ILLEGALL

proof of
your tiny
brain.
~~these~~
Vandal was
molly watkins.

Wednesday, October 25

I finish casework early
to have movie night
with Dad.

↑ Admission
of poor
work
ethic.

�֍ Thursday, October 26 ✳

Movie night cancelled.
Dad had business trip.

✳ ✳ ✳ ✳ ✳ ✳ ✳

Jimmy Weber pays me for
solving TP case. I tell him I
don't deserve it for so little work.
I give money back. ✳

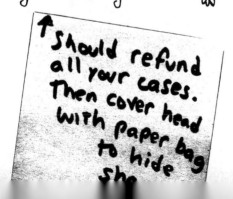

Should refund
all your cases.
Then cover head
with paper bag
to hide
sho

I search the entire log for references to me.

But there are none.

The closest I can find is a reference to Rollo.

Monday, October 30

✿ ✿ ✿ ✿ ✿ ✿ ✿

The weird kid in our group makes us all fail the test.

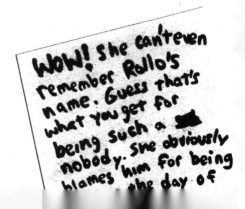

WOW! She can't even remember Rollo's name. Guess that's what you get for being such a ▬ nobody. She obviously blames him for being the day of

And that's when it hits me. What this log really is.

A plant.

No, not that kind of plant. A scheme. A ruse. A setup. To wit: All detectives know that when a company wants to hide its dirty secrets, it keeps two sets of books. The sanitized one they want the police to see. And the real one.

Knowing I'd go to Rollo's house, she purposely planted the sanitized one in her backpack in the hopes that I'd read it and see no references to me. Then I'd conclude she had nothing to do with the theft of the Failuremobile!

So now I just need to find the real one.
The one that looks like this:

CHAPTER 38

Darkness on the Edge of My Foldout Bed

I am awakened by sniper fire. I rush to look outside. It is Molly Moskins throwing pebbles against my window.

"What do you want?" I ask.

"I was thinking we should practice the play," she says.

Earlier that day, I had brought Molly Moskins to my office to discuss the play. Now she knows where I live.

"Go away, Molly Moskins. The play's not real. I explained that."

"We should probably practice anyway," she says.

"This is not a good time, Molly Moskins. I am in possession of classified information. I cannot be standing in front of an open window." I slam the window shut and return to my foldout bed.

A clump of dirt cracks the windowpane. "What now?" I cry, rushing back to the window. "You have caused grievous property damage."

"My shoes have been stolen!" she shouts. "Internationally stolen!"

It is true. She is now in her socks.

I grab my detective log. I make a note to open a file in the morning.

And that's when I realize she is holding something behind her back.

And that's when I figure it out. First she had on shoes. Now she does not. And now she is holding something behind her back.

I make a sketch of what I know is in her hands.

"Drop it right now, Molly Moskins!" I shout. "We shall not be victimized by your spree!"

My mother swings open her bedroom door and turns on the living-room light. "Why are you yelling?" she asks.

She sees me standing in front of the window. The broken one. "And how did that happen?" she yells.

"We were the victim of a criminal mastermind," I tell her. "Be thankful. It could have been much worse."

"What are you talking about?" she asks.

"The little terror was going to tiptoe around in her socks. It's called *stealth*."

"Who?" she yells.

I point out the window. We see only bushes.

"Timmy, I had to put down a huge security deposit for this place. And you know what happens with something like this? It comes right out of that deposit."

She is incredibly unappreciative.

"First you loan out my Segway for some play without asking. Then you break the window. When are you going to learn to respect other people's property?"

I withstand the barrage in silence. I am a genius unrecognized in his own home.

"And by the way," she adds, putting her hands on her hips, "I had a little talk with your friend Rollo Tookus yesterday."

Wonderful, I thought. No good can come of this.

"He came over looking for something he said was missing from a backpack. So I asked him about this little school play."

My left eye twitches. Then my right.

"And you know what he said?" she asks.

I don't. But I am rooting for the rotund kid like never before.

"He said there wasn't one."

Subterfuge! Betrayal! I hop on my foldout
bed and shout:

My speech is bold. Defiant. Even stirring.
But then I add this:

Saturday. As in the day three days from Wednesday. Wednesday being today. It is a lie so profound and far reaching that I want to modify the bottom of my left shoe.

My mother smiles and turns off the light. And answers me from the dark.

"I'd like that very much."

CHAPTER 39

I Need Paw

We are going to storm the castle. The castle being this:

The stormer being this:

We have no time to waste. Total will smash in the door. Rise on his hind legs. And roar with an Arctic fury that makes seals weep. One thousand, five hundred furious pounds. All demanding the Failuremobile.

In polar-bear-ese.

Which may require translation.

The sign was my idea. The wording was Total's.

I didn't like it. So I nixed it for something more primeval. More beastly. More Frankenstein.

Sure, the sign lost clarity. But now it was direct. Intimidating.

My plan was to accompany my business partner to the bank. Guard the exits. But I can't.

Because I'm trapped.

In the bowling turkey's shiny Cadillac.

I am being held hostage against my will. Or, as my mother describes it, I am going to the hardware store. We are going there to get a new pane of glass. For the window I didn't break.

I have forty-eight hours to get the Failure-mobile. And none for this.

Nor do I have time for the bowling turkey's lecture. The one he's giving me about growing up. And being responsible. And not acting like a little kid.

And not playing pretend.

So at a stop sign, I kick open the Cadillac door.

And I run.

I run anywhere. Nowhere. Away.

And into the furry side of a polar bear.

Who, on his way to the bank holding a ME WANT sign, was given everything well-meaning shop owners and food vendors could possibly think to give him. So that by the time this monstrous mammal was to crash his hulking frame through the front door of Evil's head-quarters and intimidate all, he looked like this:

But I don't get mad. I take his paw. And we walk. Two against the world.

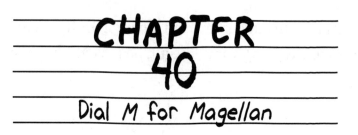

CHAPTER 40

Dial M for Magellan

You can't spell *Magellan* without an *M*.

I know that because I spelled it wrong on my World Explorers history test. Here's how I spelled it:

Chang

I answered "Chang" because the question was, "Who was the first person to sail around the globe?" And I didn't know. But I did know that Chang was the most common last name in the world. So I played the odds.

It's not the first time I've done that.

Who wrote the United States Constitution?

Chang.

The bottom line is that today is Friday. And I have twenty-four hours to find the Failure-mobile.

And unless one of these explorers is going to find it, they're of no use to me.

Though I did come close to getting the question "What were the names of Christopher Columbus's three ships?"

Huey,

Dewey,

and Louie

CHAPTER 41

Seal of Approval

"'The World's Happiest Seal thought the world was a wonderful place,'" reads my mother.

THE WORLD'S HAPPIEST Seal thought the world was a wonderful place.

"Timmy," she says, "can we stop for a minute?" She is reading one of the stories I've written for Total. But he is already asleep.

She puts down the story. "Listen. I know things haven't been easy lately. With my job and the apartment and all the changes."

I shrug and stare out the dark window.

"Anyway, I just want to say, Crispin told me about the talk he had with you," she says.

Uh-oh. Here comes the mom hammer.

"And I told him he had no right."

I look back at her.

"*I'm* your parent. Not him." She clears the hair from my forehead. "That doesn't mean it was right to run from the car. He spent two hours looking and couldn't find you any-where."

Of course not. He is an amateur. He is not going to find a trained detective.

"Anyhow, if you want, I thought maybe we could get some seafood after the play tomorrow.

I thought your business partner might like that."

Ah, yes. The play. The one I'm going to write after she leaves my room. "My business partner would like that very much," I say. "And it's wise of you. He's one half of the agency's hiring committee."

She kisses me on the nose. And gets up to leave.

"Where you going?" I ask her.

"To bed."

"But you didn't finish the story."

She smiles and sits back down. And begins reading again.

"'The World's Happiest Seal thought the world was a wonderful place.'"

She turns the page.

Boy, was he disappointed.

CHAPTER 42

Broadway Bound

"Stop touching me!" I yell at Molly Moskins. She has both arms around me. We are standing in front of the garden shed in her large backyard.

"You sure I don't hug you here?" she asks.

"No!" I shout, smelling like tangerine.

"I *knew* we should have practiced this play," she says. "If we had practiced, it would have been wondertastical by now."

"I told you, Molly Moskins. I just finished writing it two hours ago. I was up all night." I plop back down in my director's chair. Reach for my thermos of coffee. It is all that is keeping my eyes open.

Well, that and fear. My mother will be here in an hour. I convinced her the play had to be staged here instead of the school auditorium because some of the auditorium's ceiling tiles had fallen during rehearsals.

She asked me why the school couldn't just hold it on one of their fields instead of in Molly's backyard.

I told her the female lead was a bit of a prima donna and had demanded it be in her backyard. Little did I know it would prove true.

"You didn't even write a part for Señor Burrito!" she says.

"Focus on your lines, Molly Moskins."

"It's hard to focus when Señor Burrito is sad."

I look back at Señor Burrito. I should never take my eyes off her.

"And how can you write a play called *A Segway Named Greatness* when you don't even have a Segway?"

"The Segway is suggested, Molly. Not shown. It's supposed to be in the big box."

"I don't get it," she says.

"You're the owner of this shop that sells

Segways. And every day I walk by your shop and tell you how much I want one. Then what do you say?"

She looks at her script. "Uhh, 'Sorry, good sir. You don't have enough money,'" she reads.

"Perfect. Then I grab the sides of my head and yell, 'SEEEEEGGGGGWAAAAAY!'"

"What for?"

"What do you mean, 'What for?' I'm frustrated."

"Frustrated 'cause we don't hug?"

"We never hug."

"Is it 'suggested'?"

"No. Stop talking about hugs."

"Then what do we do after you yell?"

"Nothing. That's where the script ends."

"That's all you wrote?"

"*You* try writing a play in one night! You're lucky we have the sharp, witty dialogue we have."

"But I only have one line."

"Don't worry about that," I tell her. "We'll ad-lib the rest."

"What's that mean?"

"We wing it. Improvise. Say whatever comes to mind."

"I adore you!"

"What?"

"That's what came to mind."

"In the play, Molly Moskins. Ad-lib during the play. And don't say *that*. You can say anything but that."

"Okay. Uh. Hey, it's your mom!" yells an excited Molly.

"There's no mom in the play," I tell her.

"No. Coming up the driveway."

And that's when I see her. Walking up the driveway.

"Hello, Ms. Failure!" chirps Molly.

"You must be Molly," says my mother.

"Mom!" I shout. "What do you think you're doing here?"

"You said one o'clock," she replies.

"I said two o'clock."

"You said one." She takes out the tickets I had made at the copy shop.

Stupid typo. Never trust your Arctic business partner to proofread.

"Yeah, well, plays *never* start on time!" I tell her. "That's why you don't see anyone else here yet. It's rude."

"Well, then fine. I'll sit and wait. Where are the chairs?"

Chairs. I knew I forgot something. "They were crushed by the falling ceiling tiles," I tell her. "You'll just have to stand. Now, give the actors some space."

My mother looks at me funny.

I rush with Molly back into the house. "Give me your phone," I tell her. "Fast."

She hands me the phone. I call Rollo. "Get here now," I tell him. "My mom showed up an hour early."

"You said two o'clock," replies Rollo.

"I know what I said. Just get here now. And tell everyone else to get here now also."

"No one else wanted to come. It's just me."

"I told you to ask everyone in our class except You-Know-Who."

"I did. They said no. Do you want me to ask You-Know-Who?"

"Are you nuts?" I yell. "Alright, at least you get here. My mom's gotta see *someone* else in the audience."

"I can't come until two."

"Why not?"

"I'm studying with my tutor."

"The Evil One's with you now?!"

"Don't yell at me, Timmy. If you hadn't messed up the group tests, none of this would have happened."

I try to respond, but I can't. My voice is drowned out by a sputtering roar. I look out the window. And see a familiar face.

At least *someone* is dependable. I watch through Molly's kitchen window as Flo struts into the backyard. My mother spots him too. And judging a book by its cover, she moves as far away as possible from Flo the Librarian.

I return to the phone. "You listen to me, Rollo Tookus! You either get here right now or I find a way to be a part of every group test you ever take."

"You wouldn't!"

"I would."

Rollo shrieks. I turn to Molly. "C'mon. We have a play to start."

We rush out the backdoor and take our places on either side of the Segway box. I pace back and forth in front of it. As I do, I catch my mother's eye. She does not look pleased.

"'Well, I'll be,'" I declare in character. "'I sure would like to buy that Segway.'"

Molly says nothing.

"I say . . . I sure would like to buy that Segway."

Molly stands silent.

"I SAY . . . I SURE WOULD LIKE TO BUY THAT SEGWAY!" I yell.

Molly just smiles.

"Say your line, Molly," I whisper.

"Which line?" she whispers back.

"The one we talked about," I tell her.

She looks confused. So does my mother.

"The one we talked about!" I whisper through gritted teeth.

Her mismatched pupils widen. "I ADORE YOU, TIMMY FAILURE!" she yells, grabbing me with both of her arms. The force causes both of us to fall to the grass.

"What are you doing?" I yell, horrified.

"I'm ad-winging it!" she yells. "Just like you said."

"Let go of me!" I yell, rolling with her across the grass. But she does not let go. And together we roll downhill to the driveway.

Where we crash into the feet of someone rotund.

It is Rollo Tookus. And behind him, the Center of Evil in the Universe.

"WHAT IS SHE DOING HERE?!" I yell.

"She wanted to see the play," says Rollo.

"Well, get her out of here! She can't see this—"

"Timmy," interrupts Rollo, "she just wants to—"

"I don't care what she wants!" I yell. "She can't—"

"It's okay, Rollo," interrupts the Evil One. "I gotta go anyway and—"

"AHHHHHHHHH!" a woman screams. It is my mother. She is running from the Moskins' automatic sprinklers. Which have just come on all across the lawn.

"Turn those off!" I shout at Molly, who is still on top of me.

"I don't know how," she says. "They're sprinklermatical."

"Then we've got to move the box!" I yell. "The water will ruin the cardboard!"

I struggle to rise. Molly hangs on to my legs. I drag both of us through the jets of water to get to the box.

But before we can get there, the box does something unexpected.

It moves toward us.

"*ROOOOARRRRRRR,*" the box growls.

It is my business partner.

Who, unbeknownst to anyone, has been napping under the Segway box. And is now going to make up for the botched bank invasion by intimidating everyone here.

But he can't. Because he is now just a box with feet. And, as such, intimidates no one.

Except Señor Burrito.

Who, seeing the walking box, leaps out of my thermos and onto the face of Rollo Tookus.

Rollo panics and pulls the flying Burrito off his face. But the cat chases him. So he runs screaming into the garden shed and slams the wooden door.

Which causes the outside latch to fall and lock him in.

Rollo yells for my help. But I have no time. Because as I turn my head to avoid a jet of sprinkler water, I see my mother. Halfway down the driveway. "M-o-o-o-o-m!" I yell. But I can't move. Because Molly Moskins has both her hands around my ankle.

"LET GO, YOU IDIOT!" I yell at Molly. But as I say it, my left eye twitches. And Molly Moskins thinks I winked at her.

"YOU LOVE ME TOO!!!" she yells, pulling me back to the ground.

Smothered by kisses, I can only faintly hear the receding sound of my mother's car engine. Which is soon drowned out by the screams of Rollo.

"I DON'T WANT TO SPEND THE NIGHT IN H-E-E-E-E-E-E-E-E-R-E!!!"

Distracted by the scream, Molly turns to look at Rollo. I throw her arms off me and run. But the rest is a watery blur.

For I'm told that as I stood up, my business partner lost his balance. And fell onto my head.

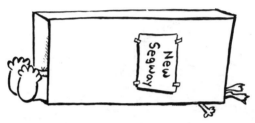

I'm further told that the same person who rescued me then unlocked the door of Rollo's garden shed prison. And scared the bejesus out of Rollo.

Who, not being a regular user of the city library, had no idea who his rescuer was.

CHAPTER
43
Kaboom

I always thought it would take one of these to bring me down:

But it didn't. It took one of these:

That's my mother. To whom, when the play ended, I was forced to confess.

Confess that I had been using the Segway.

Confess that I left it parked in front of the Hodgeses' house.

Confess that it had been stolen. And when I was done, she didn't get mad. She got silent. And with mothers, that is always the worst form of mad.

Had it been the Segway alone, perhaps I could have survived. But it wasn't. Because when she drove home that day and got the mail, she found this:

> Dear Ms. Failure,
>
> It is with regret that I inform you that your son Timmy recently scored a zero on his history exam. It is his second straight zero on an exam.
>
> Given the low marks on both these and earlier tests, we will have no choice but to have him repeat his current grade.
>
> Alexander Scrimshaw
> Principal

And that I couldn't survive. So, in a voice of deadly calm, she gave her verdict: There would be no more investigations. There would be no more cases. There would be no more Total Failure, Inc.

But that wasn't the worst part.
That was this:
There would be no more Total.

Total

That's right. To her, my polar bear was an extension of the agency. And anything and anyone connected to the agency was no more. I could fill pages reciting the arguments I made for keeping Total. But there's no point. None of them worked. Not a bit. So I called the only local place I knew that took polar bears.

And they agreed to take him.
And that left only the good-bye.

CHAPTER 44
(No Title)

CHAPTER
45
Key Worst

My destruction wasn't alone. Crocus imploded too.

Odd to see he had a first name. Most teachers don't. And it's too bad the educational system let him down. But these things happen.

Now he's stuck in Key West.

Without me.

Sure, I was a challenge. An obstacle. But old people need that.

Now he just has sun and the beach.

I can only imagine how sad he must be to get up in the morning and realize I'm not there.

But don't take my word for it. Look at the photo the school newspaper included.

He looks miserable.

CHAPTER 46

Going Against the Grain

Author's Note: The attached is an item of correspondence with my business partner. I include it here as a historical record of our time of incarceration, as well as to preserve it from the drool and food stains that would result were it to remain in my business partner's possession.

To: Total
c/o Polar Bear Exhibit
City Zoo

Dear Business Partner,

So here we are. Both imprisoned.

Your cage

My cage

How long this will last, I don't know.

All I know is that I'm chained to these textbooks from the moment I get home to the moment I go to bed...

(with a break for dinner with the warden).

Me →

← Warden

And I don't know what it is about
these books, but they appear to be
designed to send your attention
elsewhere.

Like ~~today.~~

I'm sitting there reading something
about something when I see the
pattern of the wood grain in my
desk. And before I know it, I'm
watching tiny me running through
it like a maze.

And away goes an hour.

So I try to read again. But I hear
a dog.

Which makes me think of cars.

← cars

Which rhymes with jars.

← Jars

Which hold mayonnaise.

← Mayonnaise

So now I'm eating a bologna sandwich.

And <u>two</u> hours are gone.

So I try to study again.

But my underwear is too tight.

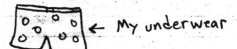

← My underwear

So I have to change it.

So I look in a drawer.

And find a flashlight.

Which still works.

So I do this.

And <u>four</u> hours pass.

Until the warden checks in.

So I run to my desk.

And say things are fine.

And look at the book.

And notice the
wood
grain.

CHAPTER 47

I Get No Kick from Kickball

"I just want to know why my hamster died."

It's Max Hodges.

And he's bothering me during lunch recess.

"I can't tell you," I tell him.

"Why not?"

"Because the investigatory enterprise has been terminated by external forces."

"I don't know what that means," he says.

"That's as simply as I can put it. I'm sorry if you don't know what it means."

"Yeah, well, I know about your play," he says, smiling.

"I see," I reply in a civil tone. "So you heard it was sabotaged by a rotund ex-associate and his evil tutor?"

He shakes his head. "I heard you fell and hit your head on a sprinkler," he says.

"Mendacity!" I shout, rising to my feet.

Max Hodges scratches his head. "I don't know what that means either," he says.

"It means I have a scalawag bent on my destruction. And she is perpetrating unconscionable falsehoods."

Max Hodges looks confused.

I attempt to walk past the ignoramus, but he grabs me by the arm. "Listen, Failure. Just tell me one thing. Without saying *how* my hamster died, can you at least tell me *if* you know."

"I'm Timmy Failure," I declare. "What do you think?"

"Right now, I think you're kind of a weirdo."

Before I can reply, I am struck in the head by a kickball.

I pick up the ball. And throw it into the street.

"Sorry about the ball, Timmy. But you didn't have to throw it into traffic."

It is the new teacher. I do not know his name. So I'll call him this:

← New Guy

"You should try playing kickball with your classmates and me sometime," says New Guy. "It's fun."

I watch as he climbs the fence for the ball. "No, thank you," I reply.

"Why not?" he persists.

"Because you are but a shadow of the man that was Frederick Crocus. And I miss him dearly."

"Aw, c'mon," he says. "Give me a chance." He tosses me the ball.

It strikes me in the face.

"You have struck me in the face again!" I shout.

"Sorry about that," he says. "Let me show you how to catch this thing." But his lecture is mercifully interrupted by the bell for class.

"Well," I tell him, "now you can proceed to destroy the inside of my head as you've just destroyed the outside."

He laughs and walks off.

I feel a woman's hand on my shoulder. "Be nice," says Dondi Sweetwater. "Mr. Jenkins is a good guy."

"Not now," I tell the yard lady. "My lunch recess has been sabotaged."

"I saw," she says, picking up the vicious kickball. "Mind throwing this in the rec shed on your way to class?"

"Fine," I reply. "But hand it to me gently. I do not wish to be struck in the bean again."

She hands me the kickball.

"Oh, and take these too," she says, lowering her voice.

She hands me two Rice Krispies Treats.

"For the big guy," she whispers.

CHAPTER 48

Sign, Sealed, and Delivered

"He used it for packaging," I tell my business partner.

"Packaging."

It is Saturday. The one day of the week I am allowed to visit Total.

"He was sending some stupid bowling scores into some league office. Can you believe these idiots even have a *league*? Anyhow, the lunkhead doesn't want them bent! Like they're state secrets or something. So his tiny brain screams, 'Hmmm. Where can I get some cardboard to stiffen the package?' And so what does he do? He pulls it off the wall. And *ships* it!"

I suppose I should back up. The lunkhead we're talking about is this guy:

THE
BOWLING
TURKEY

And the cardboard we're talking about is this guy:

TOTAL
FAILURE
Inc.

Our corporation's sign. Our respected brand. Now sitting on some forgotten trash heap in Bowlingville, USA.

BOWLINGville
USA

"And listen to this. The guy mentions the whole thing after the fact. You know how? He says, 'Hey, did you still need that thing in the hall?' I say, 'Yes, I needed it.' And he says, 'Well, it's gone now.' And that's it! No apology. No noth—"

I stare over the railing at my business partner. "Are you listening to this?"

Total is staring at Staci, the female polar bear who shares his enclosure. But the only thing she likes is her beach ball.·

"Pay attention to me!" I yell. "We've got to do something. We've got to stop this menace."

Total walks toward her. But she growls. So he rolls over like he's dead.

"Forget about the woman," I yell. "Focus on the business. We need a plan."

Total curls up in a corner of the stone enclosure.

"Listen," I tell him, "I know things look bad right now. But you've got to keep your head up. Corporations go through periods like this."

Total blinks.

"Okay, fine," I tell him. "You know what? I was gonna save this to cheer you up for later. But I'll just tell you now." I pause for dramatic effect. "Guess what's two cages to your left."

He yawns.

"Seals!" I yell. "Tasty *seals*!"

← Seal

I climb the railing and point frantically to the left. "You can eat them! They're dumb and fat! Just like in the stories." But Total says nothing. So I stop yelling.

"Fine, then," I tell him. "At least this'll make you happy." I pull out the two Rice Krispies Treats from Dondi I've been saving and toss them into the enclosure. Total smells them immediately. And suddenly alert, he rises on his hind legs to catch them.

But doesn't.

Because someone quicker does.

I guess Staci does like something other than beach balls.

CHAPTER 49

You May Find Yourself Behind the Wheel of a Large Automobile

I'm driving a Cadillac.

Well, not by myself.

I'm holding the wheel while the bowling turkey works the pedals.

"I wish you wouldn't let him do that," says my mother from the backseat. "He's easily distracted."

"What's the big deal?" he says. "I'm sitting right here."

"What the heck is that thing?" I yell, turning my body to point at the world's ugliest lawn sculpture.

The car swerves sharply toward the curb. The bowling turkey grabs the wheel.

"See?" yells my mom. "He almost ran over that old man."

"What's the matter with you?" the bowling turkey shouts at me.

But nothing is wrong with me. It is the sculpture that is an offense against nature. And yet it is oddly familiar.

The Sculpture

Those inclined toward generous interpretation might say it's a goddess rising from the sea. Or Adam touching the hand of God.

I think it's a monkey throwing a chicken.

Why someone would sculpt a monkey throwing a chicken is lost on me. Perhaps it promotes monkeys. Or belittles chickens. Either way, it almost killed a man.

So the bowling turkey drives the rest of the block. And pulls the car up to a small park on a hill.

He gets out and carries a large cooler to a picnic table.

The table is filled with his bowling buddies, their bulbous bodies straining the bending benches.

I hate these Saturday bowling gatherings. I only have so much time out of my cell, and this is a waste of it.

My mother hates them too.

So she usually makes me play Frisbee.

Which I do not enjoy.

CHAPTER 50

Our Crumbling Educational System

The class is studying photosynthesis. They are hard at work.

I am in the back row trying to build the highest eraser tower ever.

"Timmy, could you please come up here for a minute?"

It is the much-too-perky voice of New Guy. And it carries with ease to my back-row desk.

The back row is where I've been sitting ever since New Guy announced we could sit wherever we wanted. The better to hide my eraser towers.

I glare as I walk up the aisle past Rollo, who now sits in the front. We haven't spoken since he sabotaged my personal and professional life.

"You got a minute?" asks New Guy as I arrive at his large desk.

"Very few, it seems. My mother has chained me to my books."

"Well, it doesn't look like you're too hard at work at the moment," he says, pointing at my eraser tower.

"I am demonstrating the effect of your photosynthesis on eraser towers," I tell him. "So looks are deceiving."

"Listen," he says, lowering his voice, "I haven't announced this to the rest of the class, but there are parts of this photosynthesis stuff that are impossible to figure out."

I am not surprised to hear this. He is an ignoramus.

"And how is that my concern?" I reply.

"I guess it's not," he says.

"Then may I return to my photosynthesis experiments?" I ask.

"In a minute," he says. "Let me just ask you something." He looks around to make sure no one is listening.

"Your friend Rollo says people pay you to figure stuff out. Is that true?"

"Rollo?"

"Yes. Your friend Rollo."

← ROLLO

stanfurd

"You mean the round fellow in the front row?" I ask.

"Yeah, I guess," he says, unsure of how to answer without insulting the round fellow in the front row.

"Well, I'm not 'friends' with the rotund boy. But yes, it is true I run a detective business that is on the verge of being a Fortune 500 company. Though at present it is shut down at the request of my interfering mother."

"I see."

"This institution is largely to blame," I remind him.

"Well, do you think if I talked to her and got her okay, you could maybe do a little research for me?"

"Fine," I tell him. "Give me a list of the topics you need researched by the close of school today. But be aware that if my mother refuses to grant permission, it will have to be an all-cash transaction. I can't risk a paper trail."

"Don't worry," he says. "I'll get her approval first."

As I return to my seat, I stare at the sea of upturned faces whose education will suffer mightily at the hands of this charlatan.

But that's their problem. Because business is business.

And it's every man for himself in this monkey-throw-chicken world.

CHAPTER 51

No Teacher Left Behind

To: Total
c/o Polar Bear Exhibit

It is a good thing my innate greatness came with humility. Otherwise, I might be tempted to brag. Instead, I'll just say this:

This week I saved the entire nation's educational system.

But I don't have time to talk about it.

Suffice it to say we have a new teacher. He is an ignoramus.

 ← Ignoramus

As such, I must figure everything out for him.

So far, I have unraveled the mysteries of the French Revolution, fractions, and photosynthesis.

Then I explained them all to him in terms his tiny brain could comprehend:

And get this:

These are all paying cases.

Well, they're *supposed* to be. He hasn't actually paid yet.

But here's the important
part:

My hypocritical mother has
<u>approved</u> of these transactions.

That's right. It looks like the
warden has finally recognized
the foolishness of shutting down
a financial empire.

But I don't have time to discuss
this.

Instead, I have to unravel the
mystery of conjunctions.

On a personal note, please refrain
from your obsession with Staci
the polar bear. In your battle
for her affections, you have lost
to a beach ball!

 ← Beach ball

Instead, focus on the reemergence of the business.

A business that may soon be needing you.

To perform an unpleasant task.

CHAPTER 52

Read All About It

I am awakened by a screaming woman.

It is the second time I have been awakened by a screaming woman this week.

My mother hands me my report on the French Revolution. There is a large *B* written at the top of it. "I can't believe it!" my mother shouts. "It's a *B*! Your new teacher gave you a *B*!"

"Our educational system's shortcomings are no cause for celebration," I tell her. "The imbecile's lucky he has me. May I return to bed?"

"And that's not even the best part, Timmy! Mr. Jenkins included a note that said you're improving in almost all your subjects! I bet if you keep it up, they'll reconsider making you repeat the grade!"

I yawn.

"Now, nothing's guaranteed, of course. I'm sure you'd still have to keep up these grades. But it's paying off, Timmy. All that studying. It's paying off!"

"I do research, Mother," I remind her. "And it's for the business. A business you all but crushed."

"Well, I don't care what you say. We need to celebrate. Let's go out to a big lunch together. Wherever you want. Would you like that?"

"I'd like to sleep in. It's Saturday."

"It's almost noon. C'mon. You'll love it."

I sit up in bed. "What I'd love is—" I stop myself.

"What?" she asks. "Say it."

"What I'd love is to get my business back."

She sits next to me on the foldout bed. "I know," she says.

"The one client you've permitted me is a deadbeat debtor," I tell her. "Who can run a business like that?"

She puts her arm around me. "Well, no promises, okay? But why don't we discuss all that at lunch?"

"Fine. At a lunch teleconference?" I ask.

"Yes. A lunch teleconference. Now, get out of bed."

I fold the bed into the couch and walk into the kitchen. I am greeted by a bowling turkey.

"Hear we're going for a big lunch, kid," he says from behind a newspaper.

"Afterward, we can head out to the park to see my bowling pals," he says. "How's that for a day?"

I reminisce about those glorious Saturdays.

"Just give me about fifteen minutes to wax

the car," he says, getting up from the table. "Then we can leave. Want the paper?" He holds out the newspaper.

"No," I tell him.

"No, *thank you,*" he corrects me. And lays it in front of me anyway.

I watch as he leaves the apartment, his polyester pant legs swooshing against each other. The door slams shut behind him. And that's when I see it. The most disturbing newspaper headline of all time.

Not disturbing enough for you?
Behold the family member.

CHAPTER 53

Where Evil Resides

I immediately understand everything.

First she gets her father to make a cash contribution to the zoo.

Then they get the polar bear exhibit renamed.

Then she gets my polar bear.

It is all as clear as the sheen on the bowling turkey's Cadillac. The same person who stole my Failuremobile is now going to steal my business partner.

I rush out of the apartment to find the bowling turkey. "I want to go to your stupid picnic now!" I yell.

"What?" says the bowling turkey, buffing his car's precious fender.

"Your picnic thing. At the park. I love it. Let's leave now."

My mother is standing next to him. "You don't want to go to lunch?" she asks.

"No!" I shout. "The picnic! I love the picnic!"

She pauses. "Fine," she says. "I'll get my purse." She stares at me with one eyebrow raised as she walks back into the apartment building. She returns with her purse. The bowling turkey opens the front passenger door for her.

"No, no. Not her. Me," I say, stepping in front of her. "I want to sit in the front seat."

"Why you rude little—" the bowling turkey starts to shout at me. My mother stops him.

"It *is* his day," she says.

"Fine," he says, "but you're not steering again, kid, if that's what you're thinking."

"I know," I tell him. "I just like to sit in front. I love it when it's all clean."

He stares at me for a moment, then throws the buffing rag into the trunk. "Okay," he says. "Get in."

We begin driving. At a stoplight, he puts the car in neutral and revs the engine. "She sure does love being waxed," he tells me, referring to his inanimate car. "Listen to that engine."

I stare at his foot pushing the accelerator.

He pops the car into drive. The Cadillac's wheels screech down the street. A street we didn't take the last time. "This isn't how you go to the park!" I yell. "Go the way we went before."

"What do you care?" asks the bowling turkey.

"It's *my* celebration!" I remind him.

He looks back at my mother.

"I guess it is his celebration," my mother says apologetically.

"Fine," says the bowling turkey. "How'd we go there last time?"

I indicate the way. He follows my direction.

And a block from the park, I see it. "Stop the car!" I yell.

"What now?" he yells.

"That house with the sculpture!" I shout. "There it is!"

"Not this again," my mom says from the backseat.

"What the heck is it with you and that stupid thing?" says the bowling turkey. "Get over it, already."

"It's just ugly," I say, staring out at it. "It ruins the look of the whole house."

"Weirdo," he says.

I see my mom frown in the rearview mirror. I'm not sure at whom.

We drive up the hill to the park. "Don't park here," I tell him. "Park there." I point to the spot on the other side of the street where we parked last time.

"You're really pushing it, kid. You know that?" he says.

"I just like to do everything the way we always do it," I tell him.

He takes a deep breath and swings the car into the spot across the street.

"Everyone's gotta carry something," says the bowling turkey, opening his trunk. He grabs a cooler and a six-pack of Coke and hands my mom a folding chair. He closes the trunk and locks the car.

"You take this," my mom says to me, handing me the soda.

"I can take more stuff than that," I tell both of them. "Give me the keys and I'll make a few more trips."

The bowling turkey stares at me.

"It's the least I can do for being such a pain on the way over," I say.

"Fine," he says, tossing me the keys. "But don't rest anything on the trunk. You'll scratch it."

I wait until they've walked through the park gate and out of view.

And hurl the soda cans to the ground.

With the sound of hissing carbonation receding behind me, I sprint toward the house at the bottom of the hill.

I stop at the edge of its front lawn.

And grab the Evil One's detective log from my back pocket.

And turn to the last page.

And there it is.

The sketch of the art piece she did for our school's open house.

The same one that's now on her front lawn.

I have found it. The fortress. The citadel. The home of the person who will not be stealing my polar bear.

I run back up the hill toward the Cadillac. Shaking, I open the car door and jump into the driver's seat. I try to recall everything I saw the bowling turkey do on the drive over.

First step, ignition. My hands fumble through the ring of keys. I find the right one. I put it in the ignition. And turn the key.

The engine roars to life.

Second step, the gas pedal. I reach my leg down as far as it will go and push it with my foot.

The engine revs as it did at the stoplight. Only deeper and louder.

Parked on this side of the street, I can peer over the steering wheel and just see the doomed house that lies straight ahead at the bottom of the hill. I need only pop the car into gear and give it the slightest of gas.

I rev the engine again.

I am entranced by its roar.

CHAPTER 54

We've Got To Fight The Powers That Be (at the Bottom of the Hill)

But I don't act. I can't. I'm just one half of a team. A man without backup. A man without muscle. I must get Total.

←—Total

I think about taking the car. But no. Can't risk it. Straight down a hill? Sure. But through town to the zoo? No way.

I hop out of the car and run for the zoo.

But I stop at the edge of the block. It won't work. That bear is trapped behind a twenty-foot moat. *He can't jump twenty feet.* He can't jump a can of beans.

Can
of
beans

Then it hits me.

Not the can of beans. Something better.

I turn on my heels and run for the school.

Where I see the Saturday soccer games.

I run through three different games until I find the one I need.

I sprint for the woman standing at its center.

"What are you doing?" Dondi Sweetwater asks me. "I'm officiating a game."

"I need the goods!" I tell her.

"The what?" Dondi yells.

A kid dribbling the soccer ball brushes past me. "The *goods*!" I remind her.

"Oh," she says, ducking under a kicked ball. "Why do you need some now?"

"Never mind that," I cut in. "I need them."

"Okay," she says as a boy smashes into her thigh. "Look in the red cooler over there. I have a box of them. I was saving them for the kids here, but—"

I don't hear the end of the sentence. For I am struck in the face by an assassin's soccer ball.

Dazed but conscious, I boldly stay on my feet and run for the sideline.

Where I find the red cooler. And grab the goods.

And sprint for the zoo.

But I have no money for admission. So I duck under the ticket window. And rush for the Arctic mammal section. There, asleep in the corner, is Total.

I tear open the box of Rice Krispies Treats and hold two high over my head.

I watch across the wide moat as Total's nose twitches. And his right eye opens. And his left.

Then he rises on his hind legs and roars.

And is pushed down with one paw by Staci.

Who still manages to hold the beach ball with her free hand.

Staci growls for the Rice Krispies Treats. Total cowers and retreats toward the far wall of the enclosure.

So I do the only thing I still can. Which is to grab the entire box and hold it high over my head.

It is a volume of Rice Krispies Treats that Total has never seen before.

And he explodes like a cannonball.

Straight across the hard stone floor of the enclosure.

Over the swimming pool.

Past the left side of Staci, who drops her beach ball as she sees:

Total leaping over a twenty-foot moat.

Before I can stop him, he is using both paws to scarf down the treats, wrappers still on.

"Eat on the way!" I yell. "We have work to do!" I hop on his back and ride toward the park, tossing treats in his mouth along the way. It is the fastest I have ever seen him run.

We run past the Evil One's house. Up the slope toward the park. Straight for the gleaming Cadillac.

Total dives into the backseat. I turn the ignition and rev the engine. And pop the car into gear.

It explodes down the hill.

This is for the CCIA.

Past the parked cars.

This is for the theft of my cases.

Past the green lawns.

This is for the Failuremobile.

Up and over the curb.

This is for Total.

And through the living-room window.

In a thunderous explosion of brick and wood, metal and glass.

The car comes to rest at the foot of a living-room table. Steam hisses from the Cadillac's broken radiator.

As the smoke from the debris clears, I peer through the shattered windshield. But I do not see the Evil One.

I turn back to Total. "We are in the correct house, right?" I ask.

He says nothing.

I look back through the large hole in the wall, where the now-shattered sculpture lies on the lawn. "That's the sculpture," I say. "This *has* to be the house."

I scan for any sign of the Weevil Bun. I see none.

And then I hear a voice from the backseat. "Why are you doing this?" Total asks.

"What?" I say.

"Why are you doing this?" I hear again.

"Why am I doing what?" I answer.

"Why are you doing this?"

CHAPTER 55

Guess Who's Coming To Dinner

It is my mom. And she is angry.

"Why are you doing this?!" she yells.

I am behind the wheel of the Cadillac. It is parked at the top of the hill. The engine is on. And I have not driven it anywhere.

"So this is why you wanted the keys?" she asks. "To rev the engine?"

I can see Crispin running toward me from the park gate. "What in the—? What do you think you're doing?" He reaches in and turns the engine off.

"I just wanted to hear that sound again," I tell him. "The one you made at the light."

"See?" my mom yells at him. "This is what you get. Letting him grab the wheel. Showing off with your stupid car."

"This is what *I* get?" he yells back. "You're the one that coddles him."

"Coddles him?"

"Coddles him! Why do you think he still plays all the pretend games? I'm just trying to teach him to be a man!" He turns the key in the ignition. The car roars back to life.

"Rev the engine, kid! Go for it!"

"You're ridiculous," my mother yells at him. "This has nothing to do with being a man!"

Crispin opens the passenger door and sits beside me. "You want to hear the sound I made at the light?" he says to me.

"Turn the car off, Crispin!" shouts my mother.

"Go ahead! Put it in neutral and rev the engine! It's okay. It won't go anywhere."

I put it in neutral and rev the engine.

"Stop it, Crispin!" my mom yells.

"Now pop it into drive, kid. C'mon! I've got one foot over the brake! The tires will squeal. C'mon, now!"

"I don't want to," I tell him. My left eye twitches.

"You gonna be a little kid your whole life?" he shouts at me. "Pop it into gear! I got the brakes! Pop it into gear!"

My mother runs for the driver's door. Just as Crispin pops the car into gear.

But he doesn't slam on the brakes.

Because he falls out his open door.

"TIMMMMMY!" my mother yells as the car thunders down the hill. Crispin jumps to his feet and starts sprinting for the car.

But it's too late. The Cadillac is tearing down the hill. Headed like a missile toward the home of Corrina Corrina. I strain with my right foot to hit the brakes but I slide off the seat and under the dashboard. I curl into a ball. And brace for the impact. . . .

But what happened next I don't know.

Because all I remember is waking up in a cloud of smoke and hearing the sound of adults trying to climb through the large hole in the wall.

And looking out through the cracked windshield at a plastic-covered recliner and a person sitting in it. A person eating a TV dinner.

And it is then that I have a moment of clarity.

Of Corrina Corrina.

And how she kisses up to people in authority. And gives them gifts.

Like ugly handmade sculptures they can put on their lawns.

Such as the one she gave to this guy.

The man sitting across from me.

Freshly back from Key West.

CHAPTER
56
Trouble in the Red Zone

There's not much to tell you about the police station. Except it was the last time my mother and I saw this guy:

THE BOWLING TURKEY

Only he didn't look like that. He looked like this:

11668
CITY POLICE

He's in trouble for reckless endangerment of a something-or-other. Cops grilled him bad. Really rattled the poor stiff. Not me. I've seen the inside of so many police stations I can practically walk 'em with my eyes closed. All comes with the job. And I knew the boys in blue would insist on calling me Detective Failure. So I tried to put them at ease.

The chief asked me to give a quick statement about the crash. So I did. No frills. No hysterics. Just the facts. I knew how these G-men liked it.

When I was done, I took a quick swig of the chocolate milk they gave me (all out of scotch, they said) and told them to go easy on

the bowling turkey. Poor guy's just misguided,
I told 'em.

Afterward, they offered me a tour of the
station. Didn't really want it. But I humored
them.

We walked past the booking desk. Past the
holding cells. Through the cops' break room.

It was nice. But nothing to write Mom
about.

Until we got to the impound lot outside.

And found something to write Mom about.

I recognized it by the scratch I'd given it
when I crashed into Rollo one time.

"How'd you get this?" I asked the lieutenant who was giving me the tour.

He glanced at the tag hanging from the handlebars. "Parked in a tow-away zone," he said.

I thought back to the Hodgeses' curb. Sure, it was red. But no self-respecting cop would do a tow-away job on a detective's vehicle.

"That can't be," I told the lieutenant. "This vehicle was stolen. Stolen and brought here. Probably by someone this high." I held my hand four feet from the ground.

"An elf?" he asked, making himself laugh.

← Elf

"This is no joke, Lieutenant. She's a girl. Black hair. Ethics of a mule."

"I don't know anything about that," said the lieutenant.

"I saw the vehicle!" I insisted. "Behind a bank! It was contraband!"

The lieutenant shook his head. "Kid, I don't know what you're talking about. These things all look alike." He walked back toward the police station.

"You don't understand!" I shouted.

"Thanks for your time," he said, closing the back station door behind him.

"It's a cover-up!" I yelled.

But he was already gone.

CHAPTER 57

For Whom the Timmyline Tolls

"The only reason I told your mom there wasn't a play was because *I didn't know* you were doing one. You never told me."

It is Charles "Rollo" Tookus. Standing outside my apartment window. And we are sorting through unfinished business.

"And I didn't *bring* my tutor to the play.

She insisted," he said. "And besides, how about what *you* did on all those group tests and with the bank safe and—"

"Whoa, whoa, whoa," I tell him. "The bank safe was your fault."

"Fine," he answers. "But not the group test."

I can tell he's looking for an apology. So I give him one.

"Mistakes were made," I say.

Rollo smiles. "Friends?" he asks.

"Let's not get soft," I tell him. "Come on up. I want to show you my new—"

But my answer is cut short by the crack of a sharpshooter's bullets against my window. I dive below the windowsill with lightning-quick reflexes.

When the shooting ends, I look out the window.

And see Molly Moskins.

Holding Hershey's Kisses.

"Kisses for my love!" she shouts up at the window.

"Leave me alone, Molly Moskins!" I yell. "You've terrorized this town enough!"

"But I have cases!" she yells, throwing me another Hershey's Kiss.

It strikes me in the eye. "Ahhhhh! Look what you've done! You've blinded me!"

Blinded

"Blinded you?" she asks. "Are you sure? So you can't see this?"

She lifts the cuffs of her pants. She has bare ankles.

"Someone stole my socks!" she yells.

 ← NO SOCKS

"Someone *globalnational!*" she adds.

But I don't have time to answer. Because there's a knock at the apartment door.

I open the door and see Rollo.

"How's your eye?" he asks.

"Not good," I tell him. "It feels as though she's damaged the fibula."

"That's part of your leg," he says.

"You know nothing," I tell him.

"So what did you want to show me?" he asks.

"Follow me," I say.

As we walk, I hear more Hershey's Kisses ping against the windowpane.

"So my mom cleared out all her clothes,"

I tell him, showing him my mother's bedroom closet. "She says I can use it for now. She'll keep her stuff somewhere else."

"It's smaller than the last one you had," he says.

"Of course it's smaller, you idiot. I *wanted* it smaller. My mom says I can't do as much detective work as before. Downsizing sends the message that I'm listening to her."

"Oh," he answers.

"Besides," I tell him, "I'm still missing my business partner, so the payroll's cut by fifty percent."

"Hey, speaking of that," Rollo asks, "did you ever give my tutor back her detective log?"

"No," I said. "But my mother did. She found it in the backseat of the Cadillac and returned it to the Weevil Bun's father."

"Did you read it?"

"'Course I read it. Waste of time. All personal stuff. I'm sure it bored her father to tears."

He started to ask another question. But I couldn't talk to him anymore.

Because the Timmyline was ringing.

CHAPTER
58

Elementary, My Dear Gunnar

"You're late," says Gunnar. "I called you half an hour ago."

"Could not be helped," I tell him. "Forces beyond the corporation's control have forbid further use of the Failuremobile."

"Yeah," he answers, laughing, "I heard it got towed and your mom had to pay some big fine to get it back and—"

"It was stolen, you imbecile! Stolen! I saw it with my own eyes behind the Evil One's headquarters."

"There's more than one Segway in the world, Timmy."

"Is that why you called me here? To waste my time?"

"Relax, Timmy," he says. "I just wanted to know what happened to my case. You never figured it out."

"Oh, I didn't?" I answer knowingly.

"Well, did you?" he asks.

So I proceed to lay out all of the evidence. Step by step. With clockwork precision. His brother Gabe's room. The empty pumpkin. The chocolate smeared around Gabe's face. The alibi.

"So it was Gabe?" he asks as I finish.

I try not to laugh. "Gunnar," I say, "do you remember all the candy you told me was missing?"

"I think so."

"List it," I tell him.

He thinks back. "Okay, uh, there were two Mars bars, a Twix, uh, seven 3 Musketeers, five Kit Kats, eleven Almond Joys, and, hmmm, five Snickers, an Abba-Zaba and uh . . . "

I stop him. "Say this last part slow."

He stares at me with the dull eyes of an amateur. "Eight Hershey's Kisses?" he says.

"Bingo," I tell him.

"Bingo?" he asks.

"Bingo," I say.

CHAPTER 59

Total Victory

"Are you ready?" my mother yells from her bedroom.

I'm reading the mail on the kitchen table. "What's this one?" I ask, holding up a postcard.

"We're gonna be late," my mom says, walking into the kitchen. "We've already postponed this lunch reservation once. Do you want to celebrate your grades or not?"

"It's from Crocus," I tell her.

"I know," she says. "He got a lot of insurance money for his house. So he sold it and moved."

I read the back of the postcard.

"Well, now, that's immature," I say, putting down the card.

"Are you ready or not?" she asks, "We're gonna be—"

She is cut off by the squeal of a truck's brakes. I stare out the kitchen window at a large, nondescript truck.

Large, nondescript truck ←

The driver gets out and walks toward our apartment building. I meet him halfway up the walk.

"You Timmy Failure?" he asks, checking a clipboard.

"I am he," I tell him. "The owner of Total Failure, Inc. I presume you have a case."

"A case?" he says. "I don't got a case."

He swings open the truck's large roll-up door. "I got a bear."

Total leaps from the back of the truck and knocks me to the grass. It is an unprofessional display of affection, licking, and drool.

I hug him back.

"Zoo says he don't play too good with others. Guess he did something to make some other bear real mad."

Total runs back into the truck.

And returns with something to show me.

CHAPTER 60

It Begins Again

My mother said our lunch was to celebrate grades. But that was a ruse. The truth was we were there to celebrate the rebirth of Total Failure, Inc. For I had brilliantly solved all my cases.

The Tiny Person who'd TP'ed the Weber home? Molly Moskins.

The larcenist who'd lifted the load of candy? Molly Moskins.

And the cause of death for the Hodgeses' hamster? Elementary, my dear friend. Hamsters are rodents. Cats kill rodents. And who owns a cat?

That's right. Molly Moskins's Señor Burrito is a murderer.

Other than that, I really don't want to talk about the celebration lunch because the whole thing pretty much got ruined.

For one thing, my mom made me invite Rollo. That was stupid because his GPA had recently slipped to 4.55 and his head was shaking like the top of a pressure cooker.

Then there was Total.

My mom let me order him halibut. (It was the closest thing we could find to seal.) But what a waste. The poor slob spent the entire lunch behind the restaurant.

To top it all off, we saw Flo. Eating alone at the lunch counter.

That was okay with me. But not for my mom. To her, he's still that "strange guy at the play." And I have to admit that he *did* look intimidating. Especially given the fact that he was reading another book on how to kill things.

But what destroyed the entire event—made my blood pressure rise and my fists clench— were the two people in the back corner booth. One was You-Know-Who. I'll just put the little black box over her head again.

And the other was her father.

My mom said they were coloring a kids' menu together. I didn't see that. But I did see she was smiling and laughing.

Which could only mean one thing. . . .

She was plotting more evil.

A Prologue That Will Most Likely Make Sense Later

Of all the items that can clog your plumbing, an overweight Arctic mammal is probably the worst.

Because while a good plumber can clear your pipes of a spoon or a hair ball or a bar of soap, it is much harder to remove one of these:

That, you see, is a polar bear.

And today he is stuck in a different kind
of pipe.

The Tube O' Terror.

Tube O' Terror

The Tube O' Terror is the world's fastest,
curviest waterslide.

But it is not fast today.

Because it is clogged.

Clogged by an overeager polar bear who
was much too plump to ride.

And yet somebody let him.

And that is where the bribery comes in.

Because a polar bear who fails to get his way will charm. And a polar bear who fails to charm will deceive. And a polar bear who fails to deceive will grab a big wad of dollar bills from his pocket and wink.

Because that is how the world works.

And then this will happen.

CLOG

And if you are a world-class detective who just so happens to be tied to that polar bear and had no choice but to follow him down the slide, you are in trouble.

Deep, unbreathable trouble.

Because the rushing water keeps coming.

And with the polar bear's big bottom acting as a plug, the water has nowhere to go but back up the tube.

Which is where I am.

Trapped underwater.

And not very happy about it.

CHAPTER
1
A Head Is a Terrible Thing to Not Have

Carl Kobalinski is not the smartest person in the world.

But try telling that to the woman in the checkered vest.

"Maury's Museum of World Records is now closed," she says. "And you need to go home."

"But look at this thing," I tell her. "It's an outrage."

"What is?" she asks.

"This," I say, pointing directly at the statue.

"Kid, I get eight dollars an hour to walk around this museum and make sure no one breaks anything. If you have a problem with what's in it, tell someone else."

"I've got a problem, all right. Lies, lies, and more lies. Everyone knows who the smartest person is."

"Wonderful," she mumbles, rubbing her temples.

"It's me," I say.

"Good for you," she says, pushing me toward the exit with one hand. "Now let me show the smartest person in the world how a door works."

I am suddenly tempted to pull rank.

Reveal that I am this guy:

Timmy Failure

Distinctive Scarf

It is a name so recognizable that she would instantly know it as that of the founder, president, and CEO of the greatest detective agency in the town, probably the state. Perhaps the nation.

But I don't pull rank.

I do something smarter.

I climb Carl Kobalinski and try to yank down his sign.

"What do you think you're doing?" screams the museum woman.

"I'm saving the credibility of your institution!" I retort.

But I'm not.

Because I can't reach the sign without jumping. And I am nine feet above the ground.

So I do what only the smartest person in the world would think to do.

I jump.

Only to learn that while Carl may have had a strong brain, his statue does not have a strong neck.

And as I jump, it snaps. Sending both me and Carl's overrated head tumbling.

Straight to the museum floor.

Where I hear another snap.

This one in my leg.

And say the only logical thing I can to the museum woman leaning over me:

"Now look what you've done."

CHAPTER 2

The Cast That Limits Me

When you're lying in bed with a broken right leg, you can either cry or write your memoirs.

And Timmy Failure doesn't cry.
So here are my memoirs:

I was born.
I exhibited greatness.
I founded an empire.

And that empire was achieved despite the many obstacles around me.

Such as Obstacle No. 1.

That's my mother.

She's a kind enough person. But she has her weaknesses.

Like insisting I attend this place:

Now, school is fine for those who need it.

But for those touched by greatness, it is a debilitating nuisance.

Then there's Obstacle No. 2.

His name is Total. He is a fifteen-hundred-pound polar bear.

He was raised in the Arctic. But his home melted like an ice cube in the sun. And he wandered 3,000 or so miles to my house.

So I gave him a job.

And for the first six months, he was the most reliable polar bear I've ever employed.

Then he revealed his true colors.

It was a betrayal so profound that I do not wish to discuss it.

So let me just say this.

If a polar bear ever works very hard for you in the first six months of employment, keep this one thing in mind:

IT IS A RUSE.

Do NOT make him a partner at your detective agency.

Do NOT agree to change the name of the agency from "Failure, Inc." to "Total Failure, Inc."

And, hey, while I'm issuing warnings, do NOT model your life after the person who is Obstacle No. 3.

His name is Rollo Tookus. He is my best friend. And he is boring.

Boring because all he cares about is grades.

So that's all the description he gets.

And I will fill the space he otherwise would have gotten in these memoirs with a drawing of my face.

CHAPTER 3

Drags Like Butter

When you are one of the world's high-profile detectives, you can expect your fair share of high-profile cases.

And the one I get this morning on the Timmyline is about as high profile as it gets.

The call is from a classmate. Nunzio Benedici.

And he is missing something precious.

"I can't find Spooney Spoon," he says.

"Don't panic," I tell him. "I'll be there in twenty."

And I don't necessarily mean minutes. It could be hours.

Because of this thing I've had on my leg the past couple weeks.

← Cast

Which means I can't walk fast.

Now, that wouldn't have been a problem when I had the Failuremobile.

← Failuremobile

That was a Segway I borrowed from my mother.

But then my mother sold it.

So then I had the Totalmobile.

Totalmobile

That was a wagon pulled by my business partner.

But then my mother sold it (the wagon, not the business partner).

So now I just let my business partner drag me through the streets on a rope.

Which may seem difficult.

But it's not.

Because I coat myself in butter.

So now I have the Buttermobile.

CHAPTER 4

Veni, Vidi, Benedici

(I Came. I Saw. I Ran Into Nunzio Benedici.)

As if I need to tell you, Nunzio Benedici is the kid in my class who can shove the most eraser tips in his nose.

← Nunzio Benedici

And Spooney Spoon is the spoon he uses to eat his applesauce.

Spooney Spoon

Don't ask me why there's a dog's head on it. I don't know.

And I won't ask.

Because if there's one thing you learn in this business, it's that clients have their secrets. Each more shameful than the last.

So when I arrive at his house, I stick to the basics.

"Prepare for a three-month investigation," I tell him. "And perhaps some international travel."

"International travel?" he replies.

Naive clients. The bane of a detective's existence.

"Spoon Larceny 101, kid. When a spoon goes missing, the first thing they do is ship it over the border."

"I didn't know," he says.

"There's a lot you don't know," I tell him. "That's what you pay me for."

"How much will it be?" he asks.

"Four dollars a day. Plus expenses."

"Expenses?" he asks as he reaches into his pocket for change.

But as he does, he sneezes.

And I am hit by a hundred eraser tips.

"Dry-cleaning my scarf," I say. "Your first expense."

CHAPTER
5

I Know Why the Caged Bird Doesn't Sing

Eraser tips are not the only menace in my life these days.

There is also my great-aunt.

Who right now seems far from great.

I say that because she has attached wheels to her shoes and run into the birdcage.

And now she's unconscious.

I'd help her, but it's the second time today. And fourth time this week.

Which is something I know because I live with her.

I suppose I should explain.

My mother, my polar bear, and I used to live in an apartment. But my mother lost her job.

So we had to move in with my mother's aunt Colander.

A colander is the thing you use to drain spaghetti.

Colander

I'm not sure how she got that name.

Perhaps it is because she has holes in her head through which her brain cells escape.

Brain cells

All I know for sure is that she once had a husband, Great-Uncle Gustav.

Gustav

But then he died. Possibly to escape Great-Aunt Colander.

GUSTAV
R.I.P.

Escaped

But Gustav was rich. And when he died, he left my mother's aunt with a big mansion in the big-mansion-filled town of Santa Marinara.

Now, that should be enough for any great-aunt. But it's not.

Not enough

Because Great-Aunt Colander believes she has not yet made her contribution to the civilized world.

That, she believes, is this:

THE BOOM BOOM SHOEWHEEL

The Boom Boom Shoewheel is a set of two wheels that you attach to each of your shoes.

It is not a roller skate.

The difference, as Great-Aunt Colander will explain to you for the better part of an afternoon, is that a roller skate *already comes with a shoe.*

Shoe

The Boom Boom Shoewheel does not.

No Shoe

That is apparently too subtle a distinction for sporting-goods stores, all of whom refuse to carry this dangerous product and refuse to take any more phone calls from Great-Aunt Colander.

I only wish *I* could get away from her that easily.

But I can't.

So the best I can do is enjoy some of the perks that come with a mansion.

Like the fact that my detective agency is now housed in its largest office to date.

My great-aunt's solarium.

It's spacious. It has great views. And the glass offers protection.

Against the wind.

The bees.

And the occasional flying aunt.

CHAPTER 6

Spoon Rollo Anthology

Flying aunts or no flying aunts, the Nunzio Benedici case will not wait.

So I have traveled again to Nunzio's house. And I'm conducting a lineup.

"Stand still," I say to Rollo Tookus. "This is official police business."

"I have a book report due," says Rollo.

"And don't talk," I tell him. "It's distracting."

I turn to Nunzio.

"Okay, Nunzio. Is this the fellow you saw take your favorite spoon? The one you call Spooney Spoon?"

"Rollo?" says Nunzio. "Of course not. All he ever does is study."

I make a note of that in my detective log.

I look back at Nunzio.

"So if I understand you correctly, you think Rollo took Spooney Spoon."

"That's not what I said," says Nunzio.

"Well, I wish you would," I say. "He's the only guy I could get to come over."

"That does it," says Rollo. "I'm going home."

"Look what you've done," I yell at Rollo. "You've intimidated the witness."

"I'm not intimidated," says Nunzio.

"Fine," I tell him. "We have more suspects to go through anyway."

But we don't.

So I grab anyone I can to parade in front of Nunzio.

"Is this the fellow you saw take your favorite spoon?"

"I keep telling you," says Nunzio. "I didn't see anyone take Spooney Spoon."

"Good," I say. "It gets complicated if I have to arrest my own business partner."

"Look," says Nunzio. "For the last time, all I know is that Spooney Spoon is missing."

"All right, all right, calm down," I tell him.

"I am calm," he says. "You're the one who's sweating all over my bedroom carpet."

I laugh with confidence.

"The CEO of the nation's finest detective agency doesn't sweat, Nunzio."

"Then what do you call that?" he says, pointing at my forehead.

"Butter," I say. "Lots and lots of butter."

CHAPTER 7

One Flew Out of the Cuckoo's Nest

Even quick-witted professionals such as myself need time to solve international heists.

But Spooney Spoon will have to wait.

Because of another flying distraction.

My great-aunt's lovebird.

Torpedo Bob.

 ← TORPEDO BOB

Torpedo Bob was named for his reported propensity to escape from his oft-damaged cage and dive-bomb random targets with a malicious intensity rarely seen outside of war.

And right now, his cage is empty.

← EMPTY

"Darn it, Timmy. I don't have time for this," says my mother. "I have a job interview in ten minutes."

"Get Great-Aunt Colander to find him," I tell her. "It's her fault for always crashing into the cage."

"And how am I supposed to do that?" my mom asks, pointing at the unconscious Great-Aunt Colander.

Unconscious

"So help me look for the silly bird," says my mom.

But I can't.

Because the Total Failure Alert goes off.

POP POP POP

The Total Failure Alert is a high-tech alarm system developed by Total Failure, Inc., labs to warn agency personnel of impending doom.

It consists of three sandwich baggies.

Three baggies

A set of these is distributed to each Total Failure employee upon completion of basic training. (Known as Achieving Baggie Privileges.)

While the manner in which a threatened employee utilizes the alert is both highly technical and legally patented, I shall try to explain it here:

Employee fills baggies.

Employee pops baggies.

But don't get bogged down in the technical details.

Because the important part is this.

An employee may **ONLY** sound the alert when one of two life-threatening situations is happening:

> 1. the world is ending; or
> 2. the WEDGIE is present.

The WEDGIE (face blurred for your protection.)

WEDGIE stands for:

Worldwide
Enemy of
Da
Goodness
In
Everything.

And she is just as uncomfortable as that other kind of wedgie.

Narrator's demonstration of that other kind of wedgie *

* Extreme variety wherein underwear is pulled up so far it can be stretched over head.

In her long and sordid past, the Wedgie has gone by many nicknames (the Beast, the Evil One, the Weevil Bun). But I'm not going to go into it.

Because we're not going to talk about her.

Suffice it to say that when I hear the Total Failure Alert, I know it can only have come from one individual:

My business partner.

And wherever he is, he is in trouble.

Life-threatening trouble.

So I hobble toward the sound of the alert.

Down a long hallway. Up a flight of stairs.

Through an arched doorway.

Into old Gustav's study.

Where I find this guy:

Hiding from this guy:

Meaning that this guy:

Has lost his Baggie Privileges.

CHAPTER
8

When the Moon Hits Your Eye

Mr. Jenkins is making an announcement.

He is my teacher.

But I'm not listening.

Mostly because I am taping Rollo Tookus to his desk.

"What are you doing?" he whines. "I want to hear what he's saying. It sounds interesting."

"School is never interesting," I say, preparing to tape down his free hand.

"But he's announcing a contest," he says.

"And I'm doing a science project. I call it Our Friendly Universe."

"Can I please hear this?" he says.

"Now, listen," I tell him. "You're the sun. So you're stationary. Hence, all the tape."

"Oh, great. He just said the deadline. And I didn't hear it."

"And I'm the earth," I continue. "So I'll circle you like I'm in orbit, though that could be difficult with a broken leg."

I limp around Rollo to demonstrate my orbit.

"You're blocking my view," he says.

"Do you mind if I paint you orange?" I ask him.

"Paint me *what*?" Rollo says.

"I want to play!" squeals a girl.

It is Molly Moskins. The girl who ruins everything.

← MOLLY MOSKINS
(Ruins everything.)

The reason she ruins everything is that she smiles too much and she smells like a tangerine.

Plus, she has one pupil that is bigger than the other and has no respect for personal space.

"Give us room, Molly Moskins. I'm on the verge of a Nobel Prize."

But she doesn't give us room. She runs closely around me.

"What are you doing?" I yell.

"I'm the moon!" she chirps. "And I run around you while you circle around Rollo."

"Will you two please shut up?" asks Rollo.

"That's absurd," I say to Molly. "For one thing, you're carrying a Hello Catty lunch box. The moon would never carry a Hello Catty lunch box."

I try to push her away while I limp around Rollo.

"I love my Hello Catty lunch box!" she shouts as she waltzes around me.

"I'm getting dizzy," cries Rollo.

"WHEEEEE!" cheers Molly Moskins, now running with her eyes closed.

"I'm getting nauseous," complains Rollo.

"What do you three think you're doing?" barks Mr. Jenkins.

Whose voice surprises the moon.

Who runs right out of her orbit and into the sun.

Who falls on the earth.

Who careens into a storage closet.

The entire universe has collapsed.

"Well, I hope you're happy," I tell Mr. Jen-kins. "You've discouraged three kids who were otherwise very interested in science."

CHAPTER 9

Ousters and Insults and Bears — Oh, My!

"All in favor of ousting the bear from the board, please raise your hand."

I raise mine.

Total does not.

We are at loggerheads.

This is how all the board meetings of Total Failure, Inc., go.

The only difference now is that we hold the meetings in a huge room. My great-aunt's dining room.

349

"You're lazy. You're a glutton. And you run from small birds," I tell him.

This is how all our meetings end. With personal insults.

Total leans back to reply. But his chair collapses.

"And how many times do I have to tell you not to lean back in that chair? You're a thousand pounds over its capacity."

My mother barges in from the kitchen.

"Blame the bear," I tell her.

"Did Aunt Colander say you could play in here?"

"No one's *playing*. It's a board meeting. And if you interrupt again, I'll have to ask my security detail over there to escort you out."

I point at Total.

Total yawns.

"Timmy, why didn't you show this to me?" she asks, holding up a piece of paper.

"I don't even know what it is. But if you're going to interrupt the meeting, you could at least say, 'Point of order.'"

"Point of order, then. It's a notice from your school. It was in your backpack."

"You're rifling through my papers? At long last, ma'am, have you no sense of decency?"

"It says that the school's holding a detective contest. You should enter."

I grab the sheet of paper from her hand.

"Is this a farce?" I ask.

"It's a contest, Timmy. It sounds fun."

"Fun? It's a personal insult. They *know* who the greatest detective is."

"Nobody's trying to insult you, Timmy. It's just a game."

"It's not a game, Mother. It's a direct shot at me, the agency, and my global reputation."

"Oh, my goodness," she says, leaving the room. "I'm sorry I showed it to you."

Total follows her out. The gluttonous bear follows anyone who walks into the kitchen.

"This slander shall not go unanswered!" I declare to the boardroom. "All in favor of proving that Timmy Failure is nobody's fool?"

But the room is empty.

So nobody seconds my motion.

"Motion passes," I declare.

CHAPTER 10

Timmy vs. the Red Baron

Principal Scrimshaw's office is a serious place. So I have worn a serious hat.

"Timmy, I don't know what to tell you," he says. "It's a contest. No one's making fun of you."

But I can't hear him.

Because my hat came with a biplane that circles around it.

RRRRRRRRRRRR

"You'll have to speak up," I tell him. "The plane is loud."

"It's a contest!" he shouts. "No one's making fun of you!"

The plane recedes behind my head.

"Relax," I say. "You can talk normally now."

"Timmy, I have a lot of things to do. If you want to enter, enter. Your submission needs to be into this office on Friday. My secretary, Marilyn, can give you the exact time."

"Absurd," I reply. "That's three days from now. I can solve your mystery right now."

"Yeah, well, it's not *my* mystery. It's the district's. So you'll be competing against entries from all of the other schools as well. And whoever turns in the most well-written and thorough solution will win."

"How sad for the other students," I say. "Do they know that they're competing against a professional?"

"I don't know what they know, Timmy," he says, putting on his suit jacket. "But you need to go, because the teachers and I have our monthly meeting with the superintendent."

"Just one more thing," I say.

"Hurry," he says, stopping in the doorway.

"I think we both know that I bring

tremendous star power to your contest. So the question is obvious. What's in it for me?"

"Oh, good gosh," he says. "I'm leaving. Marilyn, see that he leaves my office."

His secretary walks in. She smiles.

Marilyn, the Smiling Secretary

"All that money's not enough for you, Timmy?"

"What are you talking about?"

"I'm sorry," she says. "I couldn't help eavesdropping. The winner gets money."

"The winning detective gets money?"

← Money

"Yep," she says.

"How much?"

"Five hundred dollars."

"Five hundred *dollars*? That's a fortune!"

"Well. No. But it's a lot."

"The agency could go global! I could open that office in Peru!"

"I like your enthusiasm," she says.

"This isn't about enthusiasm. It's about the start of an *empire.*"

"I see," she says.

"With Timmy Failure at its head!"

"Wonderful!" she says.

"Because Timmy Failure is nobody's fool!" I shout.

To which she says something something something something.

None of which I hear.

Because the biplane comes back.

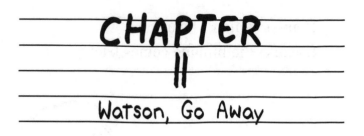

CHAPTER 11

Watson, Go Away

Holding hands is the second worst thing in the world.

The worst is holding hands with this person.

"I'm not even supposed to be using this leg," I shout.

"I see you hobbling around on it all the time," replies my great-aunt.

"Mendacity!" I shout.

"Mendacity!" she repeats. "I like that word."

"I should be in bed right now. Recuperating."

"No, you shouldn't. You love the museum."

The museum she's talking about is this place:

The same place I got this:

Broken leg

"I wish you had never introduced me to that place," I say. "It's a factory of lies."

"Mendacity!" she shouts, almost losing her balance.

"See why we have to hold hands?" she adds.

"All I know is that Carl Kobalinski is a moron," I tell her.

She grabs on to a passing tree for a rest. "Boom boom stop," she says.

"Boom boom stop" is something she says each time she stops on the Boom Boom Shoe-wheels. As though holding hands with her isn't embarrassing enough.

"You're probably right," she says.

"Right about what?"

"That Kobalinski fellow. What case did *he* ever solve?"

"Exactly," I say.

"A real genius solves cases," she says. "Like Sherlock Holmes."

"Well, Holmes had his weaknesses," I remind her. "But yes, we detectives are the true geniuses of the world. Which is why I'm about to crack the biggest case of my generation."

"The missing globe?" she asks.

"How'd YOU know about it?"

Missing globe

"The flyer. Your mom left it on the dining-room table."

"In plain view?"

"Right next to a broken chair."

"I know nothing," I say.

"Mendacity!" she shouts.

She smiles and begins skating again. This time without the hand-holding.

"I don't care about the chair, Timmy. But I do have an idea."

"What's that?" I ask.

"That Sherlock Holmes fellow. Didn't he have an assistant?"

"Watson," I say.

"Watson," she repeats.

"What about him?" I ask.

"Me," she says. "I can be your Watson."

I almost choke on my tongue.

"Absurd," I bark. "You have absolutely no training."

"You could give it to me!"

"Wrong. No chance. I already have an able assistant."

"And who is that?" she asks.

I think of Total. And the last time I saw him. Stealing supplies from the Buttermobile.

"I don't want to discuss it," I tell her.

"Oh, relax," she says. "It was just an idea. Besides, there's the museum."

She points at the block ahead.

But as she does, she loses her balance.

And I grab her hand.

CHAPTER
12
A Penny for Your Tots

It's amateur hour in Kiddieland.

And the pro sits back and sighs.

"What are you doing in the Tater Tot tray?" asks Rollo.

"What are you doing in the cafeteria?" I ask.

"You're the one in the Tater Tot tray."

"It's called *surveillance.* Besides, this sneeze guard offers protection against attack. Now go and play pretend with the other detectives."

"What other detectives?"

"As if you don't know."

"I don't."

"Half this school is running around like bumbling ninnies trying to solve a case they have no hope of solving, and you know nothing about it?"

"You mean the missing globe contest?" he asks. "I'm not doing it."

Finally. A concession to my greatness. I reach under the glass to pat him on the head.

"There, there," I say. "There's no shame in admitting defeat. It's not your fault you were born in the Timmy Failure era."

"I was born in the era of having to get good grades," he says. "And the contest doesn't affect your grade-point average. I asked."

Poor kid. He still thinks grades are important.

Little does he realize how five hundred dollars will set you up for life.

"Yeah, well, you get your good grades,

Rollo. But do me a favor. Be my eyes and ears in this joint. I don't want anyone trying to game the system."

"Game the system?"

"Bamboozle. Hoodwink. Con. Defraud."

"I get it."

"Deceive. Swindle. Sucker. Fleece."

"I get it!" he shouts, shaking his large round head. "I'm just saying I think you're a little paranoid if you think someone's gonna cheat on a school detective contest."

"Paranoid? *Paranoid?* There's not one person in this county, much less this state, who stands a chance against me in this contest. So naturally, I have to guard against the one thing that can bring me down. *Shenanigans.*"

"Shenanigans? Timmy, not everyone has to cheat to beat you."

"Ha!" I yell. "Are you a loon?"

"No, I'm not a loon. I think we both know at least one person in this school who has a chance."

"Say it and you'll ruin my entire day."

"Say what?" asks Rollo.

"I'm telling you, I'll get right on my Buttermobile and leave."

"What are you talking about?"

"The name, Rollo. She Whose Name Shall Not Be Uttered. I don't want it cluttering my large focused brain."

"Ohhh," he says. "You mean Corrina Corrina?"

Name uttered.
Brain cluttered.
Head buttered.

CHAPTER 13

Welcome to the Monkey House

Because big-mouth Rollo opened his big loud Rollo mouth, you are now going to want to know all about You-Know-Who.

So fine.

Here you go.

This is Corrina Corrina (aka the Wedgie).

And below is how she is described in our school yearbook. (Feel free to skip over it. It is a cornucopia of lies.)

> Corrina Corrina is an honors student and has won a number of academic awards. When she is not in school, she likes to work in her detective agency, the Corrina Corrina Intelligence Agency (CCIA).
>
> The CCIA is headquartered in a former bank building. The building is located downtown and is well stocked with the latest high-tech detective gear!
>
> Corrina Corrina has a good reputation for solving cases and is well liked by her classmates.

Okay. This is me, Timmy, again.

And everything in the above section is a big fat garbanzo lie.

First, not one person likes Corrina Corrina.

Second, she has never solved a case.

And third, she has the ethics of an organ-grinder's monkey.

Organ-Grinder's Monkey

Moreover, a number of pertinent details have been left out. Namely:

- Corrina Corrina is the subject of hundreds of ethics complaints that have been filed with the Better Detective Bureau.[1]
- She is a felon.[2]

---

1. I have filed all of them.
2. She once stole my Failuremobile, though the police claim I parked it in a red zone and got it towed away. That account is pure propaganda.

And last but not least:

• She may be Satan.

CHAPTER 14

'Twas the Night Before Greatness

It is the night before the contest deadline.

Amateurs everywhere are preparing their entries.

And I am lying in bed designing the Lazy Bear 2000.

"I don't care if you don't like it," I tell my business partner. "Because we're installing it."

The Lazy Bear 2000 is a high-tech device designed by me to monitor my partner's work activity.

It looks like this:

And it works like this:

1. A high-definition camera spies on my business partner.

2. The information from the camera is sent to a computer, which determines whether or not my business partner is being lazy or gluttonous.

LAZY

GLUTTONOUS

3. It also notes when he is being responsible or industrious.

┌　　　　　　　　　　　　┐

No photo
on file

└　　　　　　　　　　　　┘

4. If either of the latter conditions is satisfied, the Lazy Bear 2000 spits out one chicken nugget.

SPROING

The
Lazy
Bear
2000®

But Total is raising one objection after another.

The product's name.

The invasion of privacy.

The small food portion.

He is also threatening to punch the Lazy Bear 2000 until it spits out *all* of its chicken nuggets.

"It will be made of bear-proof steel," I tell him. "So good luck."

"Good luck with what?" I hear back.

I look up and see my mother. Standing in my bedroom doorway.

"Must you interrupt all my meetings?" I ask.

"The door was open. Besides, our bedrooms are too far apart in this place. I don't like having you so far away from me."

She sits on the edge of the bed and puts her arm around me.

"Finishing your contest entry?" she asks.

"I am not."

"I thought it was due tomorrow."

"It is."

"So you've finished it already?"

Oh, how I yearn for the day when my judgment is no longer questioned by the masses who besiege me.

"I have it under control, Mother. And you're coming very close to outright insulting me."

"No one's insulting you, Timmy. I just know how much this means to you."

She kisses me on the nose and places a peanut-butter cookie in my hand.

"Made them for you," she says, hugging me. "Good luck tomorrow."

"Thank you," I mumble.

And hug her around her neck.

She taps me on the nose with her index finger. "Lights-out in half an hour," she says.

I watch as she closes the door.

And turn back to look at the cookie.

The cookie that is no longer in my hand.

Thanks to a pilfering fur ball.

GLUTTONOUS

CHAPTER
15
By the Time I Get There in My Phoenix

"Can't this thing go any faster?"

"No," says my great-aunt, behind the wheel of her Pontiac Phoenix. "I'm going as fast as I can."

"This thing's gotta be thirty years old!" I tell her. "Why don't you take some of your money and buy a *fast* car?"

"Because I like this one," she says as the car sputters out.

"Fiddlesticks," she says. "Engine always goes kaput on right turns. Know a way to school that only has left turns?"

"What!" I answer as she tries to restart the engine.

But it doesn't respond.

So I hop out.

"What do you think you're doing?" she asks.

"Running for it," I say. "I'm probably five hours late for school as it is!"

"You can't run on a broken leg!"

"I can go faster than this thing," I say, pointing at the broken-down car. "The school's just three blocks away."

I grab my crutch and limp the three blocks as fast as I can.

Which is not very fast.

Because of my banner.

It was essential that I bring it. For it is the motto of my agency.

But it is unwieldy. And eventually the long stretch of cloth becomes wrapped around my head.

And I can't see where I'm going.

And am hit by a train.

"Well, hello, Timmy Failure!" squeals the train that is Molly Moskins. "You ran right into me!"

"Not *now,* Molly Moskins. I'm late!"

"What happened?" she asks.

"My mother didn't wake me! Now, please get off! I have a detective contest to enter!"

But I can see that she's not listening.

Because she's staring at my cast.

"How come you never let me sign that?" she asks.

"Because I didn't let *anybody* sign it! It looks unprofessional! Now, will you *please* get off me?"

But she won't.

Because she is sad.

"Oh, here!" I shout, handing her a piece of chalk I was going to use to color my banner.

Her eyes light up.

"But be quick!" I add, "Because this is the most important day of my life!"

Which it is.

Because today is the day I enter the contest.

And solve the mystery of the missing globe.

And win the money that will enable the agency to expand.

Into places like Peru.

Which seems a long way from where I am now.

Which is facedown on the front lawn of our school while a tangerine-scented girl draws hearts on my leg.

Soon my leg looks like a billboard graffitied by Cupid.

"Cute," says Rollo, walking up to us with a half-eaten Pop-Tart hanging from his mouth.

"Don't you have anything better to do?" I shout.

"It's lunchtime," he says. "How come you weren't in class this morning?"

"None of your business," I answer.

"Turn in your contest entry yet?" he asks.

"No!" I shout at him. "Why do you think I'm in such a hurry?"

"I dunno," he says. "But I don't think they're due until one."

"One o'clock?" I ask. "How come nobody ever told me that? All they said was Friday!"

"Dunno," says Rollo.

"That's a pretty *M,*" says Molly, signing her name.

"What time is it now?" I shout at Rollo.

Rollo looks at his Stanfurd wristwatch. "Half past noon," he says. "Looks like you have half an hour to get it into Scrimshaw's office."

"Phew," I say, relieved. "Just enough time to solve the mystery."

Molly gets off me. I unwrap myself from my banner.

"You haven't solved it yet?" asks Molly.

"No, I haven't it solved it yet. I'm Timmy Failure. That's the whole plan."

"To not solve it?" asks Rollo.

"No, Pop-Tart-head. To solve it. But not *just* solve it. To solve it with *flair,*" I explain.

"What does that mean?" asks Molly.

"It means I'm gonna go where all the kids are lining up to turn in their entries and let everyone know that I haven't even *thought* about the mystery."

"What's the point of that?" asks Rollo.

"Because they'll be stunned," I tell him. "Here they've put all this work into the stupid thing and I'm just as casual as can be."

"But you could lose," says Molly.

"Wrong," I answer. "Because while those poor kids are staring at me with their wide eyes, I'll start asking them questions. *Leading* questions. *Professional* questions. 'Did you find the fingerprints on the desk?' 'Did you interview the suspicious janitor?' And those kids will be so intimidated by my technique that they'll answer."

"They will?" asks Molly.

"Of course!" I answer. "And that's when I'll close my eyes, think about what they've told me, and solve the mystery."

"You can do that?" asks Molly.

"I'm Timmy Failure," I remind her. "I can do anything."

"But how will they know you've solved it?" asks Rollo. "You can't shout out the answer to the other contestants."

"Because," I explain to him, "as soon as

I solve it, I'll climb the school's flagpole and hoist my Banner of Greatness."

But Rollo doesn't hear me.

Because the flagpole falls.

"Brakes kaput," says my great-aunt.

CHAPTER 16

The Lying, the Watch, and the Poor Globe

I march down to Principal Scrimshaw's office as a man at the peak of his tactical power.

Like Napoleon in Austerlitz.

← Napoleon

Grant in Vicksburg.

Mario in the Mushroom Kingdom.

Only to find no mushrooms.

"Where is everybody?" I ask Marilyn, the No-Longer-Smiling Secretary.

"What do you mean?" asks Marilyn.

"The amateurs. They're not lined up. Did they get intimidated like Rollo?"

And as I say his name, I hear his voice.

"Timmy!"

He is lumbering toward me faster than he has ever run the mile in P.E.

"Must you shadow me at every key event in my life?" I ask.

"We have to talk," he says.

"Not now!" I tell him.

"Timmy," says Marilyn. "I don't know what to tell you."

"Tell me about what? I have a contest to enter. Where is everybody?"

"Timmy, my watch!" interrupts Rollo.

"Pipe down, Rollo," I answer.

"They were all here already," says Marilyn.

"The other kids? They came early?"

"Yes. Well, no. They weren't early."

"What are you talking about?" I ask.

She kneels in front of me. Her eyes level to mine.

"Timmy," she says. "It's ten minutes after one."

My left eye twitches. Then my right.

"Mendacity!" I answer. "It was 12:30 five minutes ago."

Rollo holds up his watch.

I peer at Rollo.

"It must have stopped," he says, tapping its face.

I feel the blood rushing to my head. I pivot back to Marilyn.

"This can't be!" I shout. "I'll solve the globe mystery right now!"

"Timmy, I can't," she says. "This is our school's deadline."

"The janitor took the globe! The vice principal took the globe!"

"I can't do it, Timmy," says Marilyn. "I'm sorry."

"It was you! It was Rollo! IT WAS PRINCIPAL SCRIMSHAW'S WIFE!"

At that, I see the blinds open in the office window.

Behind which is Scrimshaw.

"You can change this!" I yell at him.

Scrimshaw points at his watch. Shrugs his shoulders.

"You can change this!" I tell him.

He shakes his head.

"It's just ten stupid minutes!"

"I'm sorry," he mouths.

"Who are you afraid of?" I ask. "The

superintendent? The mayor? I have connections! We'll get them canned!"

But as I pound on the glass, I drop the Banner of Greatness, the reflection of which no longer fills the office window.

Allowing me to see deeper into the office.

To the chair in front of Scrimshaw's desk.

And the person in that chair.

Sitting smugly.

"SHENANIGANS!" I scream.

CHAPTER
17

The Entire Universe
Has Collapsed

"The deadline was the deadline, Timmy," says my mother. "I'm sure it wasn't Corrina Corrina who made your principal enforce it. She probably had a totally unrelated reason for being in his office. And besides, what good does it do to lock yourself in Uncle Gustav's study?"

"It's not a study," I tell her.

"Then what is it?" she asks.

"A grievance factory," I answer.

Before she can comment, I slide Grievance Card No. 1 under the door.

"What is this?" she asks.

"Read it," I say through the door.

"I had a job interview!" she says. "So I asked your great-aunt to wake you."

"I wouldn't have needed *anyone* to wake

me if someone hadn't fed me sugary cookies just before bed and kept me up half the night."

"So this is all my fault?" she asks.

I slide Grievance Card No. 2 under the door.

"Your great-aunt? Timmy, without her you wouldn't have made it to school at all. You missed the bus. It's not her fault her car broke down."

I slide Grievance Card No. 3 under the door.

"Okay, this is getting absurd," says my mother. "I mean, really, Timmy. Can you act any more ridiculous?"

I shove another card under the door.

"Okay. We're done," says my mother.

"We're not done," I reply.

"Right," she answers. "You haven't given me a card for your great-aunt's bird."

I think about Torpedo Bob. And the things I could probably blame him for.

"I'm not talking about the bird," I answer. "I'm talking about the rotund kid."

"Rollo?" she says. "You're going to blame your best friend?"

"Bingo," I say. "For owning a defective watch. Among a bevy of other faults."

"Wonderful," she says. "Slide me his card."

But I can't.

So I open the door.

"Stack's too big," I say.

CHAPTER 18

Getting a Head

I know that if I am to move forward like the professional that I am, I must first see the past with mature eyes.

And that means acknowledging that others have caused all my problems and blaming them for it.

But I am not yet finished.

I have one more party to blame. For the lies. For the leg. For the slowing me down.

So I travel the necessary distance to do it in person.

And once there, I let him have it.

"CURSE YOU, CARL KOBALINSKI!"

Only now he is headless.
So it feels odd.

CHAPTER 19

Last Train to Glooberville

My journey back from the museum is interrupted by Mr. Eraser Tip.

"I—I—I think I know who swiped Spooney Spoon," stammers Nunzio Benedici.

And I don't have time for it.

"Get ahold of yourself, Benedici," I tell him. "You're talking to a professional."

"I know. Sorry to track you down like this."

"Well, it better be good. I like to use my time on the Buttermobile to think."

"It *is* good," he says. "I think it was Minnie who took it."

"Who's she?"

"It's a he. And he's my cousin."

"What evidence do you have?"

"He just got sent to Glouberman."

"What's Glouberman?"

"Glouberman Academy," he says.

GLOUBERMAN ACADEMY

"Don't know it," I say.

"It's the school for—"

"WAIT," I say.

"You know it?" he asks.

"No," I answer. "I just got butter in my eye."

He waits for me to wipe it.

"Go ahead," I say.

"It's the school for bad kids," he continues.

"What'd he do to get sent there?" I ask.

"I dunno. But you have to be bad."

"Bad how, Benedici?"

"I guess acting bad in class and getting bad grades and stuff."

"And what's this Glooberville supposed to do for them?"

"Glouberman," he says. "It's a lot more strict about behavior and all that. Plus, they all get help with their schoolwork. You know, like individual tutors and more time to turn in assignments and—"

"Circumstantial!" I shout as I pull on the rope for Total to stop.

"What's that mean?" he asks.

"It means put more butter on my head," I say, handing him a cube. "I have somewhere I have to be."

"I can't," he says.

"Why?" I sneer. "You too important to help a hard-nosed detective navigate the gritty streets of an unforgiving city?"

"No," he says. "I'm lactose intolerant."

CHAPTER 20

'Cause He's a Voodoo Child

Back in school, I listen to Rollo Tookus tell me what "lactose intolerant" means.

"It means an inability to digest dairy products," he says.

"Are you sure?" I ask. "Because it sounded like something anti-detective."

"I'm sure," he says. "And will you put that thing away? It looks nothing like me."

The "thing" he's referring to is my new
Rollo Tookus voodoo doll.

ROLLO TOOKUS
VOODOO DOLL

"You sabotaged the most important day of
my life," I say, holding up the doll. "And this
is the emotional support I need."

I poke the doll in the eye with my finger.

"Feel anything?" I ask.

"No," he says.

"Give me that!" booms a voice from behind.

It is Mr. Purgatoni. Our geography teacher.
And he is holding the doll by its head.

"I have you kids in my class for one hour a week to teach you geography," he says, shaking the doll violently as he points.

"Do you feel *that*?" I ask Rollo.

Purgatoni clears his throat. "And the least you can do is pay attention."

It's true.

The school is trying a new experiment where we get to leave our regular classroom a few times a week to learn certain subjects from different teachers.

Mondays are English with Ms. Kelmsley.

Wednesdays are science with Mr. Peters.

And Fridays are geography with the guy now holding the voodoo Rollo.

I'm not sure why they picked Mr. Purgatoni to teach geography. Especially since he normally teaches wood shop. Maybe it's because he only teaches half a day and has his afternoons free.

Or maybe it's because he's the most boring person they could find.

"I would gladly pay attention if your lecture style were more gripping," I explain to Mr. Purgatoni. "As it is, I find it rather jejune."

Rollo pulls away from me.

"Jejune?" he says. "You think I'm dull?"

"Dull," I respond. "Pedestrian. But don't be discouraged. You seem like a nice man."

A hush comes over the class. Even Molly Moskins sits stone-faced.

← Stone-faced Molly Moskins

"This is a referral to the principal's office," says Mr. Purgatoni, ripping a pink sheet from a pad. The sudden nature of the gesture causes the voodoo doll to drop from his other hand and land headfirst on the classroom's hard floor.

I look over at Rollo.

"Surely you felt that."

CHAPTER
2|

There's a Place in France Where
the Wedgie I'll Surpass

The solarium is sweltering.

The mood is menacing.

And we are beset by Bingo's leaf blower.

"Will you please turn that thing off?" I yell
at Bingo, my great-aunt's gardener. "I'm in the
middle of a motivational speech."

But he doesn't hear me.

So I climb back on my chair and continue my inspirational speech to Total. Only this time louder.

"'YOU ASK, WHAT IS OUR POLICY? IT IS TO WAGE WAR AGAINST A MONSTROUS

TYRANNY, NEVER SURPASSED IN THE
DARK LAMENTABLE CATALOGUE OF
HUMAN CRIME!'"

Total rolls on his back to scratch his rear
end.

Scratch
Scratch

"'WE SHALL NOT FLAG OR FAIL! WE
SHALL GO ON TO THE END!'"

The blower suddenly stops. And I am left
shouting at top volume.

"'AND WE SHALL FIGHT IN FRANCE!'"

My great-aunt rolls in on her Boom Boom Shoewheels.

"You're fighting in France?" she asks.

"Is there no privacy in this place?" I moan.

"Because if you're fighting in France, I should go with you."

I get off my chair.

"It's from a book of speeches by Winston Churchill," I tell her. "I found it when I locked myself in the study."

"You locked yourself in the study?" she asks.

"It's like he *knew* the Wedgie," I say.

"Well, if you're fighting the Wedgie, I'm fighting the Wedgie," she says.

She pauses to scratch her hip.

"Who's the Wedgie?" she asks.

"Never mind," I answer. "And I don't need your help."

"It's always good to have allies," she says.

"For your information, I have a fifteen-hundred-pound ally on my side. He is a predator. He is feared. And he is at the top of the Arctic food chain."

But as I say this, I hear a high-pitched squeal.

And see a certain ally running.

And turn back to my great-aunt.

"When can you start?"

CHAPTER 22

A River Named Bob

I am failing geography.

Presumably for answers such as this:

> **Name the longest river in the world.**
>
> Probably already has a name. But fine, I'll call it Bob.

Ditto my English class, where Ms. Kelmsley did not approve of my book report on *The Lion, the Witch, and the Wardrobe:*

BOOK REPORT

I'm guessing the lion ate the witch's clothes.

My math class is not going much better.

> A man is traveling 65 mph on a train from Cleveland to Pittsburgh, a distance of 130 miles. The train left Cleveland at 9:00 pm. The man wants to know what time he'll arrive in Pittsburgh. What would you tell him?
>
> That he should ask the conductor.

"I don't understand what's happening," says Mr. Jenkins, who has kept me after class. "You haven't had these problems since Mr. Crocus taught this class."

Ah, Old Man Crocus. A teacher so ill-prepared for my greatness that he had to move to an island to escape it.

"Is it because of what happened with the detective contest?" asks Mr. Jenkins.

"The detective contest?" I ask.

"The missing globe one," he says.

"Oh, that?" I say. "No, no, no, no, no."

"But I heard you were upset about how you lost."

"Lost? I didn't *lose,* Mr. Jenkins. They don't announce the winner for a number of weeks."

"Well, maybe 'lost' isn't the word. I just mean how they wouldn't accept your entry."

"Ah, yes," I say. "You're referring to The Great Injustice."

"Okay," he says.

I crack my knuckles.

"Well, Mr. Jenkins, you'll learn after you live enough years on this planet that the world is just *filled* with injustice. We detectives see it more than you civilians."

"Is that so?" he asks.

"It is, Mr. Jenkins. Shenanigans abound."

"Well, I don't know if that's true, but I'm glad to hear you're not angry."

"The world's great detectives don't *get* angry, sir. They get—"

I stop myself.

"They get what, Timmy?"

"They get better grades, Mr. Jenkins. They make every effort to get—"

WHAM!

I am hit on the head by a flying envelope.

"Get down! Get down!" I scream at Jenkins. "We're under attack."

I dive on his head to protect him. We both fall to the floor.

"Must have come through that window!" I shout.

"Please get off my head," says Mr. Jenkins.

"Remain calm," I tell him.

I get off his head.

And kneel beside the offending envelope, the topside of which is blank.

Careful to not contaminate it with my own

fingerprints, I use the end of my detective-grade scarf to flip it over.

And there, on the reverse side, find some very disturbing markings.

CHAPTER
23
The Tell-Tale Hearts

"It's obviously the work of an assassin," I tell my great-aunt. "But who?"

She is examining the envelope. The one with the hearts on it.

"Was there anything inside?" she asks.

"Of course," I say. "Have my secretary pull the letter from the filing cabinet."

But he can't.

Because his head is stuck in a cereal box.

I grab the letter myself and hand it to my great-aunt.

She glances at it.

"Timmy, this isn't the work of an assassin," she says.

"Are you kidding?" I ask. "Look at it."

"I *am* looking at it," she says. "I think it's somebody who likes you."

I bang my forehead against the solarium glass.

"You see now why I don't like to hire amateurs?" I ask my great-aunt. "I should have known better. You can't even get air-conditioning installed in this sweltering house!"

"You're standing in the solarium," she replies. "It's *supposed* to be warm!"

"I have a polar bear!" I remind her.

"All right, fine, Timmy. Maybe the heat is getting to all of us. What do *you* think the letter means?"

"It's *code*. Don't you see?"

"All I see is a bunch of hearts."

"Think," I tell her. "The heart is what keeps you alive. This person is threatening that."

"They want you—*kaput*?"

"Of course! Why do you think they threw it through the window? This envelope has sharp corners. Who knows what damage it could have done?"

"I suppose."

"And they knew Jenkins was in there. So they didn't care if they took *him* out in the process."

"Oh, my," she says. "What do we do?"

"We give me time to think."

"I can do that," she says, steadying herself against my shoulder and rolling toward the door.

"Where are you going?" I ask.

"Giving you time to think," she says. "Besides, I have a board meeting to get to."

"Whoa, whoa, whoa," I say. "You're hardly on our board."

"Not *your* board, Timmy. It's for something called an entrepreneurs' fund."

"Entrepreneurs' fund? What's an entrepreneurs' fund?"

"I don't know, exactly. I think they give money to business-type folk. I'm on all sorts of boards. Charities, schools, museums, hospitals. I guess they figure that's all an old woman like me is good for. To sit there and hear boring people give long speeches."

"Hmmph," I answer. "It's hard for me to relate to the lives of boring people."

"Me too," she says.

And as she says it, she stares down at her Boom Boom Shoewheels.

I stare at them also.

And then look back up at her.

"One day you'll sell a million of those!" I blurt out.

She smiles.

"And we'll fight 'em in France!" she yells back.

CHAPTER 24

It's a Long, Long Way to Topiary

I'm watching Bingo make an elephant out of a bush.

"Why do you do that?" I ask.

"Your great-aunt likes it," he says. "She says it adds a little fun to an otherwise dull neighborhood. I like it, too. Though I'd like it a lot more if she'd pay me."

"She doesn't pay you?"

"Oh, I shouldn't say that. She eventually does. Most of the time. But it's okay. The truth is she's such a nice woman that I'd probably do it for free."

"Can I climb up there?" I ask.

"Okay," he says, "but be careful."

I climb up the ladder and sit on the elephant's back, high enough to see into the surrounding yards.

"She's right," I tell him. "Nothing but old, boring people."

"Except for the place next door," he says, pointing to a swing set. "They must have some young kids."

I stand on the elephant's back and try to find them.

"HULLOOOOOOO!" I yell.

Which startles Bingo.

Who lops off the elephant's leg.

"Please don't yell like that," he says, staring at the damaged elephant.

"Can you make a polar bear?" I ask.

But before he can answer, I hear a loud cry.

"TIMMY!"

It's my mother.

And her shout startles Bingo.

Who lops off the elephant's tail.

"Nooooo!" cries Bingo.

"Get down before you break your neck, Timmy! I want to talk to you!"

I climb down the ladder.

"Why is your principal calling me for a meeting at his office?"

I shrug my shoulders.

"Why, Timmy?" she shouts.

"Could you people *please* stop yelling?" asks a desperate Bingo, holding the elephant's tail.

Elephant's Tail

"Why, Timmy?" she says in a softer voice.

"I dunno," I answer.

"Timmy, I don't understand. I thought all these problems with your grades and every-thing were behind us. You were doing so well."

I shrug my shoulders again.

"What is it? Is it the contest? Are you still upset about the contest?"

"No," I say.

"I want you to be very honest, Timmy," she says. "Is it me? Is it about my losing my job? Losing the apartment? Not finding work? Having to move all the time?"

I think about that.

"It's all this change, isn't it?" she asks. "You don't like change. Nobody does. You can tell me, Timmy. Is that what it is? There's no shame in admitting that. Is that what's going on?"

I think about what she's saying. And look into her eyes.

"BINGO!" I answer.

And I hear a loud snip.

"ARRGGHHH!" cries the gardener.

CHAPTER 25

Stumping the Detective

"It's my head," I say to Rollo Tookus, holding up a tree stump.

"Looks like a tree stump," says Rollo.

"You look like a tree stump," I answer. "It's an extraordinary likeness."

"Who did it for you?"

"My great-aunt's gardener. He does tapioca sculptures."

"Topiary," says Rollo. "Tapioca is a pudding."

"You know nothing about art," I tell him. "I suggest you stay out of this."

"You're the one who brought it to show-and-tell," says Rollo.

"Do I have to separate you two?" asks Mr. Jenkins from the front of the class.

"Now look what you've done," whispers Rollo to me.

"Now look what *you've* done," I answer back.

"It was me, Mr. Jenkins!" says Molly Moskins, rising to her feet. "I was the one who was talking!"

"Sit down, Molly," says Mr. Jenkins.

"What are you doing?" I whisper to Molly Moskins.

"You keep getting in trouble," she says. "So I'm saving you."

"Class, if I could have your attention for a moment," says Mr. Jenkins.

Molly winks at me.

"I don't normally do this," continues Mr. Jenkins, "but I just wanted to congratulate a person in this class for receiving the only perfect score I've given on a math test this semester."

Rollo's head begins to bob back and forth like a maraca in a salsa band.

Rollo

Stanfurd

Maraca in a Salsa band

It is something that happens before any test or at the mere mention of grades.

"And the person I want to congratulate is Corrina Corrina," says Mr. Jenkins.

"Noooo!" shouts Rollo Tookus, his head accelerating even more. "We're probably graded on a curve! I could end up with a B plus! And a B plus is the worst thing in the world!"

"Calm down, Rollo," says Mr. Jenkins. "You got an A as well."

Rollo takes a deep breath. His head slows down.

"But Corrina Corrina was truly exceptional," says Mr. Jenkins. "And I wanted to give her some recognition."

"And I would like some recognition, too!" I announce from atop my desk. "Why, just look at my beautiful sculpture."

"What are you doing?" asks Rollo.

"None of your business," I answer.

"Timmy, get off your desk," says Mr. Jenkins.

"Timmy, you'll get in trouble!" cries Molly Moskins, tugging on my arm.

"What weird, secretive thing are you up to now?" asks Rollo.

"You're the weirdo!" I shout at Rollo.

"Are you going to get down from there or not?" asks Mr. Jenkins.

"Okay, okay," I answer. And I begin to climb down.

But don't quite make it.

Because I am tackled by an overprotective Molly Moskins.

Causing me, my desk, and my binder to crash to the ground.

Where my binder pops open.

And a document goes flying.

And the secret is out.

CHAPTER
26
Through a Glass Snarkily

"You're trying to get kicked out of school!" shouts Rollo Tookus to me in the boys' bathroom.

"Keep your voice down," I say as I check under the stalls for feet.

"It's all right here," he says, holding the document that flew out of my binder.

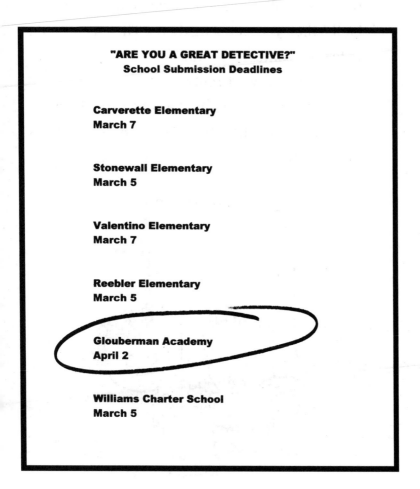

"ARE YOU A GREAT DETECTIVE?"
School Submission Deadlines

Carverette Elementary
March 7

Stonewall Elementary
March 5

Valentino Elementary
March 7

Reebler Elementary
March 5

Glouberman Academy
April 2

Williams Charter School
March 5

"I know nothing," I blurt out.

"You found out that Glouberman Academy's contest deadline is one month later than every other school's. So you decided to behave so badly that you get sent there. Then you could enter the contest after all!"

"Mendacity!" I reply.

Nunzio Benedici pushes open the door.

"OUT!" I yell, setting down my tree stump to block the door.

"It's the truth, Timmy! And it's idiotic!" bellows Rollo.

"Keep your voice down!" I answer.

The door opens again, knocking over my tree stump. "I love you, Timmy Failure!" cries Molly Moskins.

"Get out of the boys' room!" grumbles Rollo, nudging her outside.

"Timmy's my hero!" she cheers from behind the closed door.

"It's just a contest, Timmy," says Rollo, with his back pressed against the door to keep Molly out. "A stupid contest."

"It's a contest that will set me up for the rest of my life!" I snap back.

The door opens again. "I really need to go to the bathroom," says Nunzio.

"OUT!" I cry.

"Timmy, five hundred dollars does not set you up for the rest of your life," says Rollo.

"You know *nothing*," I say through gritted teeth. "*Nothing* about detective work. *Nothing* about the real world."

"Maybe," he says. "But I know your plan is stupid. And shortsighted. And even if it weren't, you don't get kicked out and sent to Glouberman just for getting bad grades and being obnoxious. Those kids are *bad*, Timmy. Very bad."

"Get out of my way, Rollo," I tell him, picking up my tree stump. "You're the reason I missed that stupid deadline."

He steps away from the door.

And as he does, it bursts open.

And he is pummeled by a flying Molly. And a flying Nunzio.

And a shower of eraser tips.

And from the bottom of that collapsed universe, Rollo cannot stop me.

Cannot stop me as I walk down the long hall with Tree Stump Timmy.

Cannot stop me as I walk toward the office of Alexander Scrimshaw.

Cannot stop me when, just outside Scrimshaw's window, I hoist the stump high above my head.

"THIS IS TAPIOCA ME!" I yell, waving the tree stump back and forth. "TIMMY FAILURE! A MAN WHO IS NOBODY'S FOOL! NOT THE WEDGIE'S! NOT THIS SCHOOL'S! AND NOT *YOURS,* SCRIMSHAW, YOU DEADLINE-FIXING, SHENANIGAN-LOVING PURVEYOR OF MONSTROUS—"

The blinds rise.

"—tyrannies," I finish.

As I see Scrimshaw.

And behind him in his office a second person.

Who I call Mom.

Whose appointment with Scrimshaw so slipped my mind that I am stunned and lose my balance.

And accidentally fall.

Tapioca Me–first.

Through Scrimshaw's window.

"Okay, now you're kicked out," says Rollo.

CHAPTER
27
Attack of the Gloubermans

Glouberman Academy has a lot of big kids.

I am not one of them.

And that can be bad. Because word is that
kids here get flattened.

Flattened

And flown.

And crammed into juice boxes.

But not me.

Because I have connections.

Like Minnie the Magnificent.

Minnie is Nunzio Benedici's cousin. And Nunzio is a client.

As a result, Minnie knows who I am. Knows my reputation. And knows that I am partners with a fierce Arctic predator.

Fierce
Arctic
Predator

As such, Minnie has tremendous respect for me. (And I, in turn, have respect for him, as shown by my giving him my lunch money every day and adding the words *the Magnificent* to the end of his name.)

This relationship has a number of advantages. For one thing, I'm losing weight. For another thing, I have time to focus on the biggest case of my life.

A case that is no longer about a missing globe. But is now about defeating injustice. And overcoming shenanigans. And obliterating the Worldwide Enemy of Da Goodness In Everything.

Which I will do.

Despite another threat on my being.

This one appeared mysteriously in my backpack.

And that was no mistake.

Because whoever did it needed to show that (1) they can still reach my person and (2) they still want me gone.

That was made even clearer by the note inside.

It doesn't take a genius to figure out what that means. Just add a couple of letters.

As in "I just missed maiming you with that last envelope."

But this time, the suspect left a vital clue.

A sticky note at the bottom of the letter.

Which can only mean one thing:

CHAPTER 28

He Sees You When You're Sinning

My mother has a long history of reacting poorly to minor incidents.

Like when I sawed through the support beams in our attic.

MY OFFICE NEEDED MORE HEADROOM.

And sledgehammered a hole in my bed-room wall.

But she has not said a word since the day I broke Scrimshaw's window.

Maybe she blames herself for suddenly appearing in the window and startling me.

Or maybe she blames Scrimshaw.

Or maybe she realizes it's all the fault of the Wedgie.

Always at fault

Whatever it is, it works for me. Because if there's one thing a detective doesn't need, it's distractions on the home front.

Particularly when he's writing his theme song.

"I like it," says my great-aunt.

"So does my Arctic business partner," I answer. "It's a compelling piece."

I play the song again.

"I particularly like how you only play one note," she says.

"Yes," I say. "It's what's known as minimalism."

My great-aunt smiles and sits beside me on the piano bench.

"Timmy, at the risk of appearing very un-detective-like, I just want to say that if you ever want to talk about things, I'm a darn good listener."

"What is there to talk about?" I say.

"I don't know," she says. "Life."

"Life?" I smirk, staring at her.

"I told you," she said. "Not very detective-like."

"Yeah, well, right now I spend every hour I have outside of the prison known as Glouberman Academy either working on the biggest case of my era or writing my theme song. So I'm not quite sure I have much 'life' to discuss."

"Right, right," she says. "I guess I just meant how you felt about everything."

"I feel fine," I tell her.

"Of course," she says. "I should have known that. Detectives are much better equipped to deal with life than normal people."

"*Civilians,* we call them."

"Yes, civilians," she says. "Like me. We civilians can have a tough go of it sometimes."

I look around her large parlor.

"Hmmph," I say. "It doesn't look like it."

"Why?" she asks. "'Cause I live in a big house?"

"A big, expensive house," I answer. "You should see some of the grim realities faced by a crime investigator on the streets."

"Oh, I imagine," she says.

"It's not pretty," I add.

She stares blankly at my sheet music but says nothing.

I look away toward the drapes.

"You okay?" she asks.

I hesitate and then swing back around to face her.

"And if *you* ever want to talk, you can probably talk to me," I blurt out.

She smiles and puts her arm around my shoulder.

"Though I would prefer it be about agency business," I add, pointing my finger at her.

She looks again at the sheet music and sings.

"GREAT TIM-MY SEES ALL OF YOUR SINS, SO DO NOT TRY SHEEE-NAN-I-GANS!"

Causing my Arctic business partner to do

the one thing he always does whenever someone sings.

CHAPTER
29
Dance Dance Revulsion

"School's not the same without you," says Rollo Tookus.

"I imagine there's great sadness," I say from atop my wounded elephant.

"I don't know about that," says Rollo. "But Molly Moskins sure misses you."

"Well, I don't miss her," I answer. "The girl has no sense of personal space."

"She wanted to come visit you also, but she doesn't know where you live and I didn't think you wanted me to tell her."

"Of course I don't. Who needs that distraction? I have one week to solve the biggest case of the millennium."

"Is that why you're sitting on a bush?" asks Rollo.

"It's an elephant. And it's where I do my best thinking."

"Oh, that reminds me," says Rollo, pulling a piece of paper out of his backpack. "Did you ever get one of these? The school handed them out a while back. It's a list of possible suspects for the globe case. I thought I'd bring you one in case you didn't have it."

> **Superintendent Dobbs has narrowed down the list of possible suspects.**
>
> **They are:**
>
> **Ms. Mabley—Reebler**
> **Mr. Purgatoni—Carverette**
> **Mr. Ryan—Valentino**
> **Ms. Kelmsley—Carverette**
> **Mr. Traynor—Stonewall**
> **Mr. Roberts—Glouberman**
> **Ms. Swann—Williams**

"Well, this is worthless," I say.

"What do you mean?"

"What do I *mean*?" I answer, pulling my hair in frustration. "You don't recognize a ruse when you see it?"

"Timmy, I don't think the school district would purposely misdirect you by—"

"Of course they would!" I reply. "Have you learned nothing from recent events? Please don't waste my time with this."

I hand him back the list.

"Fine," Rollo replies. "Figure out your own suspects. And see how wrong you turn out to be when you come to the dance."

"Dance?" I ask. "What dance?"

"Don't they tell you anything at Glouberman? They're announcing the winner of the detective contest at an all-schools dance."

"A dance! Who likes dances?"

I spot my business partner out of the corner of my eye.

"Do some work!" I snap at Total.

"And you have to bring a date," says Rollo.

"A DATE!" I yell from atop my tapioca elephant. "Can this *get* any more farcical?"

My cry is so loud that it disturbs the old man in the yard next door.

"Mind keeping it down?" asks the man. "I'm reading to my grandchild."

I get off the elephant. And point at Rollo.

"Timmy Failure does *not* go to school dances. And he does *not* bring dates. And he does *not* dance."

"Well, that's too bad," says Rollo. "Because

I figured that with the detective contest and all, you'd be going for sure. And I maybe sort of said something I shouldn't have."

"What?" I ask.

"Nothing," he says.

"WHAT?" I ask again.

"Well, a certain girl sort of thought that, well, you'd be asking her to the dance. And I sort of told her that, well, you probably would."

I stare at my round friend with a mixture of revulsion and horror.

"You didn't."

"I might have," he mutters.

I feel my head about to explode.

"And this certain girl might have already gone out and, uh, bought herself a, well, brand-new dress, just for the occasion."

"ARRRRRRGHHHHHHHH!" I yell with enough fury to be heard by the old man next door.

And the rest of the block.

And the rest of the city.

A city that contains one little girl who was no doubt staring into the mirror at that very moment.

CHAPTER 30

See You Spoon

It is high noon at the Glouberman dining facility.

And the elephants are feeding at the trough.

Including one elephant whose lunch I sub-
sidized myself.

Minnie the Magnificent. Cousin of Nunzio.
Recipient of my lunch money.

I watch as he dips his spoon into his soup.
And swallows a spoonful.

And dips in his spoon. And swallows a
spoonful.

And dips in his spoon.

And it is then that I see what is on the end
of that spoon.

A dog's head.

And as he finishes his first bowl of soup and begins a second, my detective instinct takes over.

And I realize what I am seeing.

And rush to make a note in my detective log.

CHAPTER
31
Arresting Development

There is a sculpture called *The Thinker*.

It looks like this:

← The Thinker

I am now imitating it from atop my great-aunt's fountain.

I am imitating it because I have only a few days left to think about the Biggest Case of the Millennium.

Something I used to do from atop the quiet sanctity of my tapioca elephant. Until Rollo and the old man next door ruined it with their incessant chatter.

My great-aunt's fountain is also convenient for my business partner. For him, the water is both a cool respite from the hot solarium and a shelter to hide his large body from his dive-bombing nemesis.

Well, *most* of his large body.

TOTAL'S
NEMESIS

TOTAL'S
REAR

Which is more than I can hide of my body
when I am stunned by an unwanted intruder.

"You're *The Thinker*!" trills Molly Moskins.

"What are you doing here?" I shout.

"I'm visiting my date!"

"I'm not your date, Molly Moskins. I'm not going to the dance! And how'd you even *find* this place?"

"I have my ways," she says, winking. "And you are, too, going! That's when they reveal you're the big winner!"

"For your information, Molly Moskins, I am currently making arrangements to appear *in absentia*. That means I'll be there in spirit, but not in body."

She smiles. Oblivious to my words.

"The theme is A Romantic Night in Paris," she chirps. "Paris, Timmy! Do you know where that is?"

I do, but I don't answer.

"*I* know where it is, Timmy! It's in France! The most romantic place in the universe! Should we practice our slow dances now?"

But I don't answer.

Because from atop my thinking fountain, I am once again *The Thinker*.

Thinking harder than I ever have before.

About what is going to have to happen next for me to win the contest.

So I climb down off my fountain. And walk toward Molly.

And take both of her hands.

And say the only thing I can.

"Molly Moskins, you're under arrest."

CHAPTER
32
Atlas Bugged

"You can't arrest Molly Moskins!" cries Rollo Tookus.

"What are you doing calling me on the Timmyline?" I answer. "It's for paying clients only."

"I'm calling because you've arrested an innocent person!" he says.

"Relax," I answer. "The perpetrator has been released on her own recognizance. That means she's free until trial. It was a very generous move on my part."

"Generous? Timmy, she did nothing wrong!" says Rollo.

I contemplate hanging up.

"You're really testing my patience, Rollo Tookus. But I'll try to make this simple. Molly Moskins is a criminal mastermind. A mastermind who stole the superintendent's globe. And if you think otherwise, then you—like many other amateurs—have been fooled by her duplicitous ways."

"That's ridiculous."

"You're ridiculous. *I'm* about to win a massive amount of money. And establish my agency as an international conglomerate. And make the whole world mine."

"Yeah, well, before you do all that, you need to know that the schools have provided clues to the contestants. I was going to give them to you, but I figured you'd ignore them just like you ignored the suspect list."

"La-la-la, I cannot hear you, la-la-la."

"Listen, Timmy!" shouts Rollo. "If you're going to go off and accuse Molly Moskins, you need to *hear* some of these clues. Like the fact that the globe was stolen between two and three o'clock in the afternoon. *When Molly was in class.* And the fact that it was bolted down with some special screwdriver. Which I *guarantee* you Molly doesn't have."

"La-la-la-la-la, amateur, amateur, amateur, la-la-la-la-la-la—"

"TIMMY FAILURE, YOU EITHER LISTEN TO ME OR YOU LOSE THIS CONTEST!" snaps Rollo.

I stop la-la-la-ing.

"I'm hanging up now, Rollo."

"Timmy, don't."

"I am."

"Timmy, please. I'm just trying to help."

"Perhaps. But you've crossed a professional line. And you know nothing."

"Then tell me."

"Fine, Rollo. I'll tell you one thing. One thing you must swear an oath on your ever-loving GPA to never share with anyone else."

"I swear," says Rollo.

"And if you break the oath, you will not graduate with a 4.6 GPA."

"Okay," he says.

"And you will not go to Stanfurd."

"Okay," he says.

"And you will be forced to pick up trash by the highway for the rest of your life."

"I swear! I swear, already!" he cries.

I lower my voice and continue.

"When you came to my great-aunt's house a few days ago, you said that Molly didn't know where I lived."

"Yeah," he says. "So?"

"So then she found my house and told me the theme of the dance. Which was about Paris. Which is in France."

"So?" he asks. "What's your point?"

"My point?" I answer. "My point is that you're an amateur! Do I have to draw you a picture?"

"Yeah, Timmy, I guess you do. And then maybe you should e-mail it to me, so I can be enlightened just like you."

So I ignore the snooty sarcasm and draw him a picture.

A picture of the only way Molly Moskins could suddenly have found my great-aunt's house.

And Paris, France.

That being a map.

A big, round map.

Or as some might call it . . .

A stolen globe.

And suddenly.

The whole world is mine.

CHAPTER 33

C'mon, Minnie, Light My Fire

I've had a slight bump in my professional relationship with Minnie the Magnificent. And that has resulted in a minor inconvenience.

That being that I am standing in my Mr. Froggie underwear.

Now, having your clothes taken by the largest kid at Glouberman Academy is one thing. But having it done on the day you have to explain *Bridge to Terabithia* to the rest of the class is another.

I have warned my mother many times about buying me Mr. Froggie underwear, and now the day of reckoning has come.

Fortunately, I was able to borrow a shirt from the Lost and Found office. Unfortunately, it had Hello Catty on it.

But I could not find any pants.

So I was forced to use the book itself to cover Mr. Froggie.

But that's what happens in a professional relationship when you do not hold up your end of the bargain. And hold it up I did not.

For when my mother sent me to school today, she failed to provide me with lunch money. And that meant that Minnie the Magnificent did not have lunch money.

And that meant that someone had a rumbly in his tumbly.

And that meant that someone would be staying after class.

But that is life at Glouberman Academy. And that is okay.

Because I know now that I have solved the Biggest Case of the Millennium. And that my agency is on the verge of going global. And that the brilliance of the Timmy name will soon be known on all nine continents.

So until then, I need only enjoy the camaraderie of my sometimes overzealous classmates. As I did today. When together we delighted in a spirited bonfire.

Made only slightly less delightful by Minnie's comments.

The Times They Are
A-Changin' Closet

I am shopping for a new scarf with my business partner.

And am having trouble finding just the right size.

My business partner has an abysmal sense of fashion. But I bring him anyway. Mostly because he needs a break from Torpedo Bob.

And the shopping has been productive. Because while looking for the scarf, I have found a majestic robe. One that the store will embroider with any message I want.

Which I have had them do.

Only to find that they are poor spellers.

But they offer it to me at half price. So I try it on in the dressing room.

And am disturbed by an all too familiar voice.

"You in there, Timmy?"

It is Rollo Tookus. The blight that haunts my harvest.

"Sorry to interrupt," he says from behind the dressing-room door. "But your mom said I could find you here. And I need to talk to you about the detective contest."

I swing open the door and yank him into the dressing room.

"Are you insane?" I ask. "Talking about

a critically sensitive topic like that in the middle of a public hallway?"

"Sorry," he says, looking at my clothes. "Hey, nice bathrobe."

"What do you want, Rollo? And make it quick. Your wide girth is not suited to this tight space."

"I know the solution to the contest," he says.

"Not this again!" I tell him. "I told you. I've already solved it!"

"No, no, no," he says. "You were right about all that."

"Of course I was right."

"Yeah," says Rollo. "I thought about it more, and the fact that Molly could find your house definitely means she stole the globe."

"We're crammed in here like sweat socks in a suitcase so you can tell me THAT?" I shout.

"That's not it!" yells Rollo.

"Everything okay in there?" asks a female voice. "I hear yelling."

I see the saleswoman's bright-red shoes below the door of the dressing room.

"No!" I tell her. "I need slippers to go with my robe! And please, spend as much time as you need to find just the right pair!"

"Uh, all right," she answers, walking off.

"There," I say to Rollo. "I've bought us some time. Now, hurry up before we're thrown out for exceeding the spatial limits of this dressing room."

"Fine," says Rollo. "I'll make this quick. You're going to lose the contest."

I suddenly wish I had the slippers now. So I could pummel the round head of Rollo Tookus.

"What in the name of Stanfurd University and all things you hold sacred are you talking about *now*?" I ask.

"Shenanigans," he says.

"Shenanigans?" I ask.

"Shenanigans," he repeats. "Just like you feared."

I grit my teeth.

"Start talking, Rollo Tookus."

"Well, you have the right answer to the contest. It's Molly Moskins. But it's not the answer they're looking for."

"What are you talking about?" I ask him. "What's the answer they're looking for?"

"Mr. Purgatoni."

"Purgatoni!" I cry. "That's absurd."

"Right. It's absurd. But here's what they're going to say," Rollo explains, wiping the sweat from his forehead.

"Purgatoni and the other teachers from our school have monthly meetings with the superintendent. That's where they'll say Purgatoni first saw the globe."

"Fine," I tell him. "So did every other teacher!"

"Right. But they're gonna say that Purgatoni had a motive. And the motive was that he got assigned to teach geography. And he needed a globe to learn the subject."

I see red shoes below the door again.

"I forgot to ask what size you are," says the saleswoman.

"Use your judgment!" I shout. "And please, no more questions!"

I hear the woman stomp off.

"Keep going," I tell Rollo. "I want to hear this nonsense."

"Well, then there's the window of opportunity in which to commit the crime. All the other teachers are busy teaching between two and three o'clock. But not Purgatoni. He has his afternoons free."

"Oh, what amateurs!" I cry.

"They sure are," says Rollo. "But that's not even the stupidest part. The stupidest part is the clincher they'll be relying on."

"What clincher?" I ask.

"The fact that Purgatoni also teaches wood shop. They'll say that that's how he had the means to pull this off. He's the only person who would have had the special screwdriver."

"Mendacity!" I shout. "The real perpetrator is Molly Moskins!"

"Of course," says Rollo. "It's all mendacity. But that's not what this contest is about. You said it yourself. The fix is in."

I grab Rollo by the nonexistent lapels of his Stanfurd shirt.

"How do you KNOW all this?" I plead.

He looks from side to side.

"Have you forgotten who my tutor is?"

Of course.

The biggest fly in the ointment of my friendship with Rollo Tookus.

His tutor.

HIS TUTOR
(Face once again blurred to protect your retinas.)

The Wedgie. As unprofessional and incompetent as ever. Unable to keep her mouth shut.

A low-rent detective whose loose lips will now sink her amateurish ships.

Because now I know.

The scheme.

The ruse.

The shenanigans.

So I will ignore the answer I know to be correct. And turn in the absurd one. And beat them at their own game.

I let go of my best friend's shirt and grab him by his large head.

"Rollo Tookus, your round, sweaty head contains the finest amateur detective mind in this town. Perhaps the nation. You should be very proud."

"Thank you, Timmy," says Rollo. As he is smacked on the head by a pair of flying slippers.

I pick up the slippers.

"Nope," I say. "Definitely not the right size."

CHAPTER
35
Snarl at Carl

On the day before I turn in my contest entry and establish my credentials as the Smartest Person in the World, I have a few choice words for the pretender to the title.

Headless though he may be.

CHAPTER
36
Curbing My Enthusiasm

I do not believe in omens.

But if I did, waking up to an empty cage, some scattered feathers, and a fat-cheeked polar bear would not be a good one.

Furious, I run to Gustav's old closet and grab one of his ties.

And muzzle the bear.

"That does it!" I yell at him. "That does it! I can't take it anymore! I try to be patient with you! And *this* is how you reward me? *This* is your thanks?"

Total lies down on his back. Hoping I'll scratch his stomach.

"You've jeopardized everything. *Everything,*" I tell him. "We'll be kicked out of the house. We'll have nowhere to live. What were you *thinking*?"

But the fact is that I know what he was thinking. He hated Torpedo Bob. He dreaded him. So he acted out. Reverted to his Arctic instincts.

But that's not okay when you're a detective. Detectives keep their head.

"There will be consequences for this," I tell my business partner. "Big, fat, serious consequences."

But not now. Now I have to deal with the crisis at hand. Flush the evidence. Fabricate a story. Fool the mother.

So I gather the feathers. Run to the bathroom. Flush them down the toilet.

And get ready for school as though nothing has happened.

Comb my hair. Brush my teeth.

And hear my mother yell.

"Timmy, where are you?"

My left eye twitches. Then my right.

"I KNOW NOTHING!" I yell back.

"What?" she asks, walking into the bathroom.

I glance at the water in the toilet bowl. And see a feather that didn't flush.

I slam down the toilet seat. And jump on the toilet.

"What are you doing, Timmy?"

"Morning calisthenics," I say. "I hop on the toilet. Then I flush it," I say, flushing the toilet and hoping the last feather disappears.

"Well, don't," she says. "You're wasting water. Why do you do stuff like that?"

She leans back against the bathroom counter and crosses her arms.

I say nothing.

"Timmy, we need to talk."

"I've told you, I know nothing."

"About what?"

"Nothing. I know nothing about nothing."

"Please just be normal for a second," she says, pointing at me. "And get down off the toilet."

I step down to the floor.

"First off, I don't want you to worry. Because what I'm about to tell you is my problem. Not yours."

My hopes soar. She is going to blame herself for the bird.

"In fact, from your point of view, this is probably great news."

Well, that's an exaggeration. I mean, I certainly didn't like Torpedo Bob. But I'm hardly going to celebrate his passing.

"Well, Timmy, I'll just say it," she says. "You no longer have to go to Glouberman."

"What?" I ask. "What are you talking about?"

"I got a call from the school district. It's a long story. But the short version is that the district learned we were living at your great-aunt's house. And her house isn't in the school district."

"So?"

"So if you're not in the district, you can't go to the school."

"Can't go to Glouberman?" I ask.

"Nope," she says.

"But I can go today," I shoot back. "I can certainly go one more day."

"Nope," she answers. "You can't. As of this morning, you're officially unenrolled."

"WHAT?" I shout.

"You don't have to go to school," she says. "At least until I can figure out our options."

"BUT I HAVE TO GO TO GLOUBERMAN!" I yell.

"Timmy," she says. "You can't."

"I MUST!"

"I don't understand," she says. "I thought you'd be thrilled. You hate school. Particularly that place. All you did was complain. Complain about the students, complain about—"

But I hear nothing.

Nothing but the sound of a contest I now cannot enter.

A prize I cannot win.

A universe that is collapsing.

Collapsing because of an address.

Because someone somewhere learned where I lived and felt compelled to report it to someone else.

Because that is the way the world works.

And so I lose my head.

"I GOT MYSELF KICKED OUT OF MY OLD SCHOOL FOR THIS?"

And I see my mother's face change.

From understanding.

To confusion.

To shock.

To fury.

And I limp off as fast as I can.

Out the bathroom door.

Through the house.

Through the solarium.

Into the yard.

To atop my wounded elephant.

Where I want to yell at the world.

At Carl Kobalinski.

At Alexander Scrimshaw.

At Rollo Tookus.

At Glouberman Academy.

And yet I don't.

Because I see a face.

Just over the fence.

And yell the only thing I can.

"SHENANIGANS ABOUND!"

CHAPTER 37

Tim and His Symbols

"What is it?" asks the woman in the leather chair.

"It's the Tube O' Terror," I explain, pointing at my drawing. "And through corruption and deceit, it has ceased to function."

"And what's that swollen part of it?"

"That is cloggage," I say.

"Caused by a polar bear," I continue. "A polar bear who was too plump to ride. But who, through bribery and shenanigans, was permitted to slide."

"I think that's probably enough for today, Timmy."

"And now I must suffer for it, Dr. Dundledorf. Trapped in a waterlogged tube behind a polar bear. Because that is how the world works. In case you didn't know."

"Oh, Timmy, when you talk like that, I feel like you're making so little progress."

She smiles and gets up to leave.

"The waterslide drawing is a metaphor, Dr. Dundledorf. An analogy. A symbolic tale. I can explain it more fully if you'd like."

But she has walked out of the office.

So I sit on the couch and stare at her diplomas.

Therapist This. Therapist That. Summa Cum Laude Something or Other.

And please don't ask me what a therapist is. Because I don't know.

All I know is that I come here on Mondays and draw pictures of waterslides.

And try to explain the world to her.

Unsuccessfully.

Then I think she gets paid.

If so, it's quite a racket. One I'd like in on if I ever diversify out of the detective business.

But for now I must sit.

Because of my mother.

Yes, the very same mother who responded so well when I first got kicked out of school responded less well when she found out I did it on purpose.

"I blamed myself for everything, Timmy! *Everything!* Your bad behavior! Your drop in grades! Only to find out that you were *trying* to get kicked out. All for a stupid detective contest."

And she's right.

It was stupid.

Stupid and unfair and rigged and unwinnable.

"And if those are your priorities," she added, "and you think a children's detective contest is worth jeopardizing your entire academic future—then you need *help*."

And so here I sit.

In a therapist's office.

Defeated by an unholy alliance of Principal Scrimshaw, Glouberman Academy, and the Worldwide Enemy of Da Goodness In Everything.

← Her again

And when the winner of the detective contest is announced at this Saturday's dance, it will be the Wedgie who takes home the prize.

Not through merit or brains or hard work or skill.

But the sheer power of shenanigans.

"You ready, Timmy?" asks Dr. Dundledorf from the hallway outside her office. "Your mom's in the car, waiting for you."

So I get up to leave. But pause as I pass my therapist in the hall.

"Do *you* think the world is fair, Dr. Dundledorf?"

"I do, Timmy. Not all the time. But most of the time."

I smile and nod at my therapist.

And am certain of only one thing.

She's making so little progress.

CHAPTER 38

Locust, Crocus, and My Complete Loss of Focus

For me, there is only one thing worse than leaving home for school.

And that is staying home for school.

"I don't want to be homeschooled," I complain to my mother.

"Too bad," she says, holding my math book.

"Well, what happens if you get a job?" I ask.

"I don't know, Timmy. But right now I don't have a job. So the least I can do is teach you myself."

And so we sit together for three hours a day.

And it is the longest three hours of my life.

Because during that time, I cannot daydream. And I cannot digress. And I cannot defend the agency from its debilitating demise.

All because my mother is hovering over me like a locust on a cornstalk.

"Do you have to sit so close?" I ask.

"Focus, Timmy," says my mother.

"Little did I ever think I would long for the days of my former teacher, Frederick 'Old Man' Crocus," I tell her.

OLD MAN CROCUS

"Oh, please," says my mother. "You never liked Mr. Crocus. And he never liked you."

Which is true.

He was a teacher so traumatized by his time with me that he still sends the occasional postcard from wherever he is.

KEY WEST, FLORIDA

WISH YOU WEREN'T HERE!! HA! —CROCUS

TIMMY FAILURE

But compared to the present, that all seems like a pleasant dream.

A time when I had my whole future in front of me.

And the world was mine.

But now I've lost the world. And the globe case, too.

"Cheer up, Timmy," says my mom, picking up a stack of mail. "We're done for the day. And look. You got a letter."

So I take the letter.

And see that it is from my would-be assassin.

And I throw it away.

Because I do not care.

Not about letters.

Or assassins.

Or the work of a detective.

So good-bye to that world.

And good-bye to one more relic of my glory days.

Distinctive scarf

CHAPTER 39

Stuck Inside of Santa Marinara with the Tookus Blues Again

"I got it from Scrimshaw," says Rollo. "They were going to toss it."

He is holding Tapioca Me.

"That's nice of you, Rollo," I say. "But you keep it. Use it for firewood."

He leans down to talk to me.

"How long have you been under there?" he asks.

"Days. Weeks. Years," I say. "Who knows?"

"Hey, you know, you never told me what your mom and great-aunt said about the bird. Were they mad?"

"They haven't said a word."

"Well, that's weird."

"Is it?" I ask. "Maybe they feel I've suffered enough."

"Well, I heard you're getting your cast off this week," he says. "That's good news."

"Right," I say.

"And Molly Moskins won't stop asking about you. She's really crushed you're not going to the dance."

"Right," I say.

"And speaking of which, I don't know if you're still worried about it or what, but I found out everything about You-Know-Who. Turns out that's her grandparents' house next door. She was just with them because—"

"Rollo," I interrupt.

"What?" he says.

"It doesn't matter," I answer.

"C'mon," he says. "I've never seen you like this. Let's do something to cheer you up."

He looks at the tree stump.

"Let's give Tapioca Timmy a place of prominence!" he says. "How about if I put him up high on your elephant?"

"Right," I say.

"Let's do it!" cries Rollo, struggling to lift the heavy stump over his head.

Which causes Tookus to lose his balance.

And the elephant to lose his tookus.

CHAPTER 40

Total Eclipse of the Heart

There is one last administrative matter to attend to.

So I attend to it.

"The disciplinary hearing into the bear will commence forthwith," I announce to the boardroom. "Will the director of ethics please read the charges?"

As the director of ethics, I read the charges.

"Count 1: Willfully eating my great-aunt's bird, Torpedo Bob."

"Are there any objections?" I ask.

But there are no hands raised.

Because the boardroom is empty.

As it has been for some time.

Because Total has quit the agency.

Upset about his treatment over the bird incident, he has decided that he no longer wants to be part of our corporation.

So I change the meeting's agenda.

And add one final motion.

"All in favor of telling the big, dumb Arctic beast that despite his big, dumb Arctic mistakes we maybe sort of wish he'd come back?"

I look around the room.

There is one hand raised.

CHAPTER 41

Winston Sounds Good, Like a Great Leader Should

"When you lose hope, find it."
                    —Timmy Failure

I awake to the sound of a man yelling at me.

"NEVER GIVE IN! NEVER GIVE IN! NEVER, NEVER, NEVER—IN NOTHING, GREAT OR SMALL, LARGE OR PETTY— NEVER GIVE IN!"

I open one eye.

And see my great-aunt.

"What are you doing?" I ask.

"What are *you* doing?" she asks.

"I'm trying to sleep," I answer.

"And I'm playing a record," she says, pointing at a round black spinning thing.

"It's Winston Churchill," she adds. "Your buddy."

I cover my head with the pillow.

"Let me sleep," I tell her.

"Fine," she says. "You sleep. But first, I want you to hear one more speech. And this one's from me."

She turns off the record.

"Timmy, I want to tell you something I've never even told your mother. I suspected it would come up one day when she finally asked me for money. But bless her heart, she never has. So I'm going to tell you."

She pauses and smiles.

"What is it?" I ask.

"I'm pretty much broke," she says.

"Broke?" I ask. "What do you mean?"

"It means I don't have much money."

"Well, I know what *broke* means. But how can that be? You live in this great big garbanzo mansion."

"A garbanzo's a bean, Timmy. But yes, it's all a little odd. And a little confusing. But long story short, when your great-uncle died, he put everything into what's called a trust. You don't really have to understand what that is. It just means that I don't own the house. I get to live in it, sure. But it's not really mine. So I can't sell it. I can't sell anything in it."

"Why'd he do that?"

"Oh, it's a long story. But the point is that

for years, I've lived mainly off my own savings. And that's barely enough to keep up this place."

She sits on the edge of the bed.

"So that's why I don't have a new car. And that's why I don't get air-conditioning."

I think for a moment.

"And that's why your gardener said you sometimes don't pay him," I tell her.

"Bingo," she says.

"Yes. That's his name."

"No, I meant 'Bingo,' as in 'You're right.'"

"Bingo is right?"

"Never mind," she says.

I sit up in bed.

"So doesn't all that bother you?" I ask. "Him not giving you money."

"I suppose," she says. "But not nearly as much as having to serve on all those dumb boards. That, too, was a legacy of Uncle Gustav. He recommended me to fill his seat on almost every board he was on. And I stupidly accepted."

"Boring, huh?"

"Oof," she says. "You think school is dull? Try listening to a dozen people debate the dividend rate earned on a stock portfolio for three hours."

"That is a fate worse than death," I say. "So how come you're not bitter?"

"Bitter? Who has time for bitter? I have a dream. A passion. Not much different than you. Or at least the old you."

"You're talking about the Shoewheel thingies?"

SHOEWHEEL THINGIES

"Of course," she says. "The Shoewheel thingies. And I know the whole idea seems stupid and crazy, but so do most people's dreams. And I don't care. Because it's mine. It's *my* dream. And it will remain so whether or not anyone ever wants to buy a pair."

"It's so unfair," I tell her.

"What's unfair?" she asks.

"Life," I answer. "How everyone keeps you from getting what you deserve."

"Oh, Timmy."

"I'm right," I tell her. "It's the way the world works."

She sighs.

"Timmy, listen. I know you've concluded that life is unfair. And I know people are trying to tell you that you're wrong."

"And now you'll tell me that, too."

"No, Timmy, I won't. Because I think you're right."

"You do?"

"I do. I think that life is unfair. And I know that sometimes you can't control what happens to you. And I know that sometimes those things are bad. But I know something else as well."

"What?" I ask.

"I know there's one thing you *can* control. And that's how you *respond* to all those bad things."

She rises from the bed.

"You can do what you're doing now, Timmy, and give up. It's certainly the easiest way. Or, you can fight. You can fight for what you want. You can fight for what you dream."

She stares down at me.

"Now, maybe in the end you don't get what you want. But the truth, Timmy—and maybe you haven't lived enough to realize this yet—the truth is that the beauty of life, the beauty of everything, is in that fight."

She skates from the bed to the bedroom door.

And she doesn't fall.

"So do what you have to do," she says. "And I'll love you either way."

So I wait until she has left.

And rise from the bed.

And I limp.

As fast as my stupid cast will take me.

Toward the sound.

The one made by the garbage truck at the foot of my great-aunt's driveway.

Where I find the garbageman holding our garbage can.

Which I pull out of his hands.

And dump upon the grass.

And find the one thing I need.

Distinctive Scarf,

CHAPTER 42

Timmy de Triomphe

"Doesn't my Timmykins look handsomeful?" asks Molly Moskins.

"That's not a word," says Nunzio Benedici.

"And that's the third time you've asked us that, Molly," says Rollo.

"Well, I have to talk to somebody," she says. "My date isn't speaking."

Which is true.

It's A Romantic Night in Paris. I'm in a high-school gymnasium. And I'm as silent as a basketball hoop.

"Well, I, for one, think it shows tremendous sportsmanship on Timmy's part to even show up," says Molly. "I mean, he's not even *in* the contest, and yet he's here to cheer on the winner. And that shows *class*."

Rollo looks at me. I say nothing.

"I'm surprised they even let him come," says Nunzio. "Aren't you homeschooled now, Timmy?"

"That still counts as school, Nunzio," interjects Molly.

She smiles back at me. And glances at my food.

"Aren't you going to eat your frank and beans, Timmy? Even Mr. Handsomefuls have to eat."

"I don't think he's hungry," says Rollo.

"Then I'll just save it for him for later," says Molly, taking my entire dinner setting and putting it in her Hello Catty lunch box.

"Can I have his beans?" asks Nunzio.

"No," says Molly. "You'll waste them just like you did yours."

I look at Nunzio.

He has shoved most of his beans into his nose.

"I'm going for a walk," I whisper to Rollo as I stand.

"Where are you going?" asks Molly.

"He needs to use the restroom," says Rollo.

"Okay," she chirps. "But be back in time for the first dance!"

I turn and walk away from the table.

And feel like a new Timmy.

Because for the first time in many weeks, I have no cast.

So I stroll through the gym-scented Parisian night.

Through the Arc de Triomphe.

Under the gargoyles of Notre Dame.

To the foot of the Eiffel Tower.
Where I stare up at its peak.

And think about dreams.

And the fight for those dreams.

And the beauty of that fight.

And the room goes dark.

"*Bonjour,* students! Welcome to our first-ever all-schools dance!"

A spotlight illuminates the center of the gymnasium.

Where Superintendent Dobbs stands beneath the shadow of the Eiffel Tower.

"First off, thank you all for coming. What a wonderful turnout this is. And thank you, as well, to all you supersleuths out there who participated in our Are You a Great Detective contest! Give yourself a big round of applause."

There is scattered applause.

"And yes, as promised, tonight is the night we reveal the winner. So who among you is our very own Sherlock Holmes? And who is just an Inspector Clouseau?"

He laughs. No one else does.

"But before we get to that, I'd like to

announce a very special guest. A person we've invited to the dance tonight to read the name of the winner of our contest. And I have to tell you we are honored that he is here. Ladies and gentlemen, please put your hands together for—"

"MOLLY MOSKINS!" I yell from atop the Eiffel Tower. "*SHE* IS THE TRUE THIEF!"

A sea of faces peer upward.

"Oh, good gosh!" shouts Principal Scrimshaw, who runs under the tower and stares up at me.

"My love speaks!" cries Molly Moskins.

The gym lights flicker back on.

"What is going on?" yells Superintendent Dobbs.

"SHE HAD MOTIVE! SHE HAD OPPORTUNITY! SHE HAD—"

"Get down off that right now, Timmy!" yells Scrimshaw. "Before you break your neck!"

But before I can answer, a musical note echoes out above the Avenue des Champs-Élysées.

And all heads swivel to the Left Bank of Paris.

Where a nervous Agent F sits at the school's upright piano.

Singing and playing the same repeated note.

"GREAT TIM-MY SEES ALL OF YOUR SINS!"

Scrimshaw clenches his fists and begins running toward Rollo.

Rollo spots him coming, and his large round head bobs faster than it has ever bobbed before.

"SO DO NOT TRY SHEEE-NAN-I-GANS!" Rollo quickly sings, and runs from the piano.

Scrimshaw races after him, navigating a sea of checkered tablecloths.

One of which catches Scrimshaw's foot, causing a tabletop full of plates to hit the hard gym floor with a resounding—

CRASH!

And chaos erupts.

With kids running.

And screaming.

And blocking Scrimshaw's path.

"ROLL-O! ROLL-O! ROLL-O!" they chant as Agent F flees from Scrimshaw and darts like a French bunny around an array of Parisian landmarks.

And in the frenzy of the moment, I am able to climb down the rear of the Eiffel Tower and scramble back up with the one last prop I need.

"I AM THE SMARTEST PERSON IN THE WORLD!" I shout, prop in hand.

It is a globe I have bought at a stationery store.

And it is a powerful symbol of the contest at hand.

A symbol that will resonate among the other contestants, all of whom now realize one thing. . . .

That Timmy Failure has just solved the Biggest Case of the Millennium.

"YOU'RE MY HERO, TIMMY FAILURE!" cries the felon, Molly Moskins.

But high above the chaos, I keep my head.

For I am aware, even in this impassioned moment, that there is one grand gesture remaining.

The Banner of Greatness.

A banner sure to remind both professional and amateur alike of my place in the detective world.

But a banner now lying in a crumpled heap at the base of the Eiffel Tower.

← CRUMPLED HEAP

It was to be flown by Agent F after the playing of the Timmy Failure theme, but he has forgotten.

And he is now too busy fleeing from a fuming principal.

I begin scampering down the face of the tower to retrieve it, but am spotted by a now-vigilant Dobbs, who readies himself to capture me at the base.

I do not see him until I am halfway down.

He leaps to grab me by the ankle.

But he is unaware of my lightning-quick reflexes.

And I swing my leg wildly upward. A thread beyond his grasp.

And before he can try again, I have scrambled back up to the peak of the Eiffel Tower.

"Son, you get down here *immediately*," he barks, "or I—"

But he cannot finish.

Because his threat is interrupted by an unwieldy piece of cloth whipping rapidly past his face.

It is Agent X.

Who has infiltrated tonight's event as a dance chaperone.

"WE'LL FIGHT 'EM IN FRANCE!" she yells.

And rolls on her Boom Boom Shoewheels past the Arc de Triomphe with a grace she has never shown before.

"WE'LL FIGHT 'EM IN FRANCE!" I shout back.

And hearing my shout, Agent X cranes her head back toward the sound of my voice.

And fails to see the Parisian cross traffic that is Principal Scrimshaw and Rollo Tookus until it is too late.

"BOOM BOOM STOP! BOOM BOOM STOP!" she shouts in vain as Rollo runs face-first into the banner's broad length.

Yanking my great-aunt backward.

Where she collides with a trailing Scrimshaw.

Whose momentum powers the entire trio into the side of the gargoyle-adorned Cathedral of Notre Dame.

Causing one of the gargoyles to break off and land upon the graceless pile.

My agents in peril, I do what I must.

"I WILL SAVE YOU ALL!" I shout.

And as I do, a hand grabs my foot.

"Do not move, young man!"

It is Superintendent Dobbs. And he has climbed the Eiffel Tower to get me.

"You will wait right here until someone can get a ladder and we can get you down safely! Do you understand?"

"Yes," I answer.

And as a look of relief crosses Dobbs's sweat-drenched face, I do what only the smartest person in the world would think to do.

I jump.

And see Dobbs's wide eyes.

And fall.

And see Molly run to catch me.

And fall.

And see Molly run into Nunzio.

And fall.

And see a gym full of shocked students.
And fall.
And see one more face.
Of the night's special guest.
Invited to announce the winner.
Now there to absorb—
my fall.

"*Bonjour,* Frederick Crocus."

CHAPTER 43

Scoot Scoot Scutaro

When you're lying in bed with a broken *left* leg, you can either cry or finish your memoirs.

And Timmy Failure doesn't cry.

But I can't finish my memoirs.

Because Rollo Tookus won't stop talking.

"I can't believe all you broke was your leg!"

"I fall with catlike reflexes," I explain. "It's a learned survival trait."

"And I can't believe I didn't get in trouble with Scrimshaw or the school or anything!" he says.

"Will you please quiet down and let me finish my memoirs?" I ask.

"All I had to do was tell them that the whole thing was your idea, and that you *made* me do it, and that was that."

"I didn't *make* you, Rollo."

"No, but you did make me feel responsible for everything that went wrong."

I stop writing.

"It *was* your broken watch, Rollo."

"Yeah, well, the point is that now all the other kids think I'm a hero, and none of it affected my GPA!"

The poor kid. Still concerned about things that don't matter. Like *grades*.

"Listen, Rollo, I'm pleased I could give you a taste of the detective life. A break from your routine. But remember, for me, it was just another day."

"Just another day? You knocked Crocus out cold."

"Frederick Crocus knocked himself out," I answer. "Which is what I'll say should he ever file that frivolous lawsuit. That greedy charlatan may try to gouge the justice system for all it's worth."

"Then he should sue Scutaro. He's the one with all the dough."

Oh, yeah.

I forgot to tell you that part.

A kid with the highly dubious name of Scutaro Holmes "won" the detective contest and took home the five hundred dollars.

And this is what he looks like.

SCUTARO HOLMES

From whence he came I do not know. But I have obscured his entire visage because I do not wish to give publicity to someone who is nothing more than the Wedgie's stooge.

You see, if the official account is to be given credence, Corrina Corrina (aka the Wedgie) did not even enter the detective contest.

That's right.

Did not even enter.

There are many supposed reasons for this, but let me sum them up here:

LIES, LIES, AND MORE LIES

You see, according to Rollo Tookus, the Wedgie's presence in Alexander Scrimshaw's office on that fateful day was simply to inform him that her father would be out of town for a short while. Thus, or so the story goes, she would be getting picked up from school by her grandparents, at whose house she was temporarily staying.

And because she was staying with her grandparents, she would not be near her detective office, and thus did not want to work on any cases or enter the contest.

And as if that's not enough, Rollo *also* claims that the Wedgie had nothing to do with the school finding out where I lived. That, he says, was due to my mother filling out some school form listing our address.

And if you believe all that, I have an Eiffel Tower to sell you.

So let me sum up what really happened.

The Wedgie engaged in shenanigans. The district went along at first, but after a while couldn't take the heat. And so they cracked. Convinced the Wedgie to set up a stooge. A random kid they could trot up on stage and give the cash to. Then the kid could hand the cash over to the Wedgie in some dark alley.

That way, the Wedgie could still get her dough. And more importantly, still kick back a good chunk of it to the corrupt Scrimshaw and unscrupulous Dobbs.

And no one would be the wiser.

Only she made one mistake.

She chose a kid named Scutaro Holmes. A kid with no rep in the field. And a kid who just so happens to share a last name with a very famous detective.

← THIS GUY

It is a scheme so transparent that it can only be called a farce.

But I can't talk about it anymore.

Because the Timmyline is ringing.

CHAPTER 44

A Bird on the Head Is Worth Two in the Elephant Bush

"You're lucky I agreed to meet you," I say to Nunzio Benedici. "I meet very few clients from atop my wounded elephant. It is a place of great repose."

"I just wanted to know if you solved my case," says Nunzio. "It's been a long time."

"A *long time*?" I respond. "Why, if this elephant were alive, I'd run you over right now, Nunzio. I had one leg broken by a negligent public museum. And now I have another leg broken by an old man who is incapable of catching a falling child. And you have the nerve to *lecture* me?"

"I'm sorry," says Nunzio. "I just miss Spooney Spoon."

"Fine," I tell him. "You're fortunate that I am not only skilled, but magnanimous."

"Does that mean you know what happened to Spooney Spoon?"

"Of course I know," I answer. "I'm Timmy Failure."

So I proceed to lay out all the clues.

My time spent at Glouberman. My interactions with Minnie. The spoon I saw Minnie use.

"So Minnie *did* take Spooney Spoon!" shouts Nunzio. "Just like I suspected."

I hit my elephant on the back to make him

charge over Nunzio, but the elephant does not respond.

"Will you please listen to me?" I ask. "It's bad enough you've insulted me in my place of repose."

"There's more?" he asks.

"Of course there's more."

So I take him through the night of the dance. The night of my Eiffel Tower Triumph. The night I didn't eat. The night a certain tangerine-scented girl packed up my frank and beans and put them in her Hello Catty lunch box.

"What do frank and beans have to do with anything?" asks Nunzio.

"She wanted me to *eat* those frank and beans, Nunzio."

"I don't get it."

So I draw him a picture.

Of the item she took so I could eat my frank and beans.

Nunzio stares at me.

"Just because Molly Moskins took *your* spoon doesn't mean she took *my* spoon, Timmy."

I laugh.

"Once a spoon thief, always a spoon thief, kid."

And as I say it, a bird alights upon my shoulder. As though the heavens themselves are telling Nunzio, "Timmy is special."

Until I look at the bird.

And see who it is.

And feel slightly less special.

CHAPTER 45

Sorry Seems to Be the Hardest Word to Say to a 1,500-Pound Arctic Mammal

"Mistakes were made!" I shout to my polar bear.

"BIG mistakes!" I shout. "GARBANZO mistakes!"

But Total says nothing.

"I didn't know!" I yell. "I didn't know my great-aunt had loaned her bird to some stupid charity group! I didn't know lovebirds lose their feathers! It's called *molting* or something. Who in the heck's ever heard of *that*? And how was I supposed to know you were just eating a chicken nugget when I looked at you?"

Total rolls over, his back now to me.

"Listen, if you think about it, a chicken *is* a bird," I tell him. "So technically, I wasn't really *wrong*. I was just misinformed about what *kind* of bird you were eating!"

Total gets up.

And walks out the solarium door.

I follow behind him as he crosses the back-yard toward my wounded elephant.

Where he finds the shaded spot beneath and lies back down.

I stare at him for a few moments.

And see that he is not going to respond.

So I turn to walk back inside.

But stop.

"I'm sorry," I say.

And pause to steady my voice.

"I'm just sorry."

And after I say it, there is only silence.

Followed by a loud *CRUNCH* and a massive *R-I-I-I-I-I-I-I-P*.

For Total has risen to his hind legs and torn the entire bush from the ground.

And is on me in an instant, encircling me with his big, furry arms.

The safest place I can be.

Which is good.

Because there's a gardener who wants to kill me.

CHAPTER 46

The Fix Is In

Normally, my Eiffel Tower leap would trigger a motherly meltdown. Or perhaps another visit to Dr. Dundledorf, the poor woman who is wrong about everything.

But not this time.

Because my mother is distracted.

By our move.

That's right.

After many months of searching, my mother has gotten a job.

And we're leaving my great-aunt's house.

"And I'm not very happy about it," says Agent X, skating down the sidewalk by my side.

"Well, at least she can't teach me any-more," I say. "That was truly debilitating. And I'm assuming we'll be far enough away that I never have to see that Dundledorf again. That woman is beyond hope."

"But what about us?" asks my great-aunt.

"Rest assured," I tell her. "Your position in the agency is secure. I plan on opening a satel-lite office in your neighborhood very soon."

"You do?"

"I do. I need to keep tabs on the Wedgie's grandparents. I suspect they're covert agents."

We continue down the sidewalk in silence until we arrive at our destination.

I let go of her hand to open the museum door. She steadies herself against the facade of the building.

"You're coming in, aren't you?" I ask.

"Nope," she answers. "I'm going to say good-bye to you right here. It's as good a place as any."

"Well, it's not *good-bye* good-bye," I remind her. "It's just good-bye until we come back to visit. Or I open that office. You have a very bright future."

"That's high praise," she says. "And allow me to return the compliment."

She removes a folded envelope from her pocket.

"What's that?" I ask.

"This," she says, waving the envelope, "is my reward for sitting through one boring board meeting after another."

She hands me the envelope.

"Open it," she says.

I tear it open. And pull out a piece of paper.

THE YOUNG
ENTREPRENEURS'
FUND

PAY TO THE
ORDER OF: TIMOTHY FAILURE $2,000

Two thousand and 00/100 DOLLARS

"What is this?" I ask.

"It's money. For you. From the Young Entrepreneurs' Fund. It's a group that helps kids start their own business. I'd know more, but I never pay attention in meetings."

I stare at the check. It is the most money I have ever seen in my life. And it is more than I ever could have won in the contest.

"I don't know what to say."

"Say good-bye," she says. "And nothing weepy. We're detectives, you know."

I hold out my arms to hug her.

But she shakes her head.

"You'll knock me over. Help me sit down first."

So I do.

And there I say good-bye to Agent X.

"And one more thing," she says as I walk toward the museum door.

I stop and turn.

"Your friend Rollo helped me."

"Helped you with what?"

"With a project," she says. "He's a good guy. Take care of him."

I watch as she starts to skate off. Each step a peril.

"Get in there," she says. "Before I fall and ruin this beautiful good-bye."

I turn to walk into the museum.

And am greeted at the door by the woman in the checkered vest.

"So that's your great-aunt, huh?" she says.

"You know her?" I ask.

"Nope," she says. "But I know she's on some community foundation something or other. One that apparently gives an awful lot of money to museums."

"And how do you know all that?"

"Because I'm almost as smart as you, kid. Now, are you gonna go in?"

So I hand her my money.

But she doesn't take it.

"Free," she says. "Today only."

So I enter the museum.

And take my usual path through the biggest, the baddest, the fattest, and the fastest.

And the smartest.

Fixed at last.

CHAPTER
47
It's All Downhill from Here

"Did you ever figure out who was sending you all those letters?" says Rollo Tookus, standing next to me atop the highest hill in Santa Marinara. "Because if you didn't, I could probably help."

"Great," I answer. "Is it amateur hour again?"

"Well, it's pretty obvious," he says. "And since you accuse Molly Moskins of every other crime, I thought for sure you'd figure this one out."

"It is not my fault that Molly Moskins has chosen a life of crime. But yes, I figured it out."

"You did?"

"Yes," I answer. "After I retrieved the assassin's last letter. The one I had thrown away."

"And what finally tipped you off?"

"Another sticky note at the bottom of the page. Like the one that said the assassin enjoyed M&M's."

"M&M's?" he asks.

"Never mind," I tell him. "The point is that this time the person made it somewhat clear what the MM represented."

"So you finally know who it is?" asks Rollo.

"I do."

"And are you going to try to arrest her again?"

"Her?" I answer. "Minnie the Magnificent is a *guy*."

"Minnie the Magnificent?" shouts Rollo.

"Nunzio Benedici's cousin," I answer. "He knew that Nunzio had put me on his trail. And he wanted me gone. Thus, the assassination attempt."

"I give up," says Rollo.

"You should," I answer. "You're an amateur and you get everything wrong. Now, are you going to go down this hill or not?"

I stare down at his Boom Boom Shoewheels.

"I really don't think I should do this, Timmy."

"You have to. You were her very first customer and she was so thrilled and—"

"You *made* me buy them. I didn't—"

"And," I say, holding up my index finger, "I think she'd be very disappointed if you weren't willing to use them."

"Great," he says. "So I'm the crash-test dummy. And what about you?"

"Don't be absurd, Rollo. I have a severely broken limb."

"And now you want *me* to have one?"

"Agent F, I made you an honorary member of my agency for a *reason*. Because you showed great bravery on the night of my Eiffel Tower Triumph. Please don't make a fool of me by showing cowardice here."

"I'll think about it," he says. "Can I at least have a last meal?"

"Fine," I say, grabbing a chicken nugget I'd been saving for Total.

Who smells the chicken nugget.

And lunges for it.

Causing me to yank the chicken nugget away from him.

And my arm to hit the back of Rollo.

Who begins rolling down the hill.

"NOOOOOOOOOOOOO!" yells a rapidly receding Rollo.

Who is soon far beyond my grasp.

Causing me to turn quickly back to my polar bear.

And say the one thing he needs to hear.

"*Now* look what you've done."

Timmy Failure: Mistakes Were Made copyright © 2013 by Stephan Pastis
Timmy Failure: Now Look What You've Done
copyright © 2014 by Stephan Pastis
Timmy Failure font copyright © 2012 by Stephan Pastis

First edition in this format 2017

Timmy Failure: Mistakes Were Made
Library of Congress Catalog Card Number 2012942409
ISBN 978-0-7636-6050-5 (hardcover)
ISBN 978-0-7636-6927-0 (paperback)

Timmy Failure: Now Look What You've Done
Library of Congress Catalog Card Number 2013944145
ISBN 978-0-7636-6051-2 (hardcover)
ISBN 978-0-7636-8014-5 (paperback)

ISBN 978-0-7636-9760-0 (paperback bindup)

17 18 19 20 21 22 BVG 10 9 8 7 6 5 4 3 2

Printed in Berryville, VA, U.S.A.

This book was typeset in Nimrod.
The illustrations were done in pen and ink.

Candlewick Press
99 Dover Street
Somerville, Massachusetts 02144

visit us at www.candlewick.com

visit www.timmyfailure.com for games,
downloadables, activities, a blog, and more!

TAKE A BREAK
BETWEEN CASES

Watch videos

BOOK TRAILERS

AGENCY ADS

Learn how to draw your favorite characters!

Play games

Failure is an option Blog

Free activities

Head to
www.timmyfailure.com

STEPHAN PASTIS is the creator of *Pearls Before Swine,* an acclaimed comic strip that appears in more than seven hundred U.S. newspapers, boasts a devoted following, and hit #1 on the *New York Times* bestseller list with the 2011 compilation *Larry in Wonderland*. Stephan Pastis took an unusual route to becoming a best-selling comics creator: he went to law school. Hopelessly bored sitting in class at UCLA, he found himself sketching the character Rat. Creative inspiration followed him through graduation in 1993 to his first law firm job in San Francisco, and *Pearls Before Swine* was born in 1997. The Timmy Failure series is his first creation for young readers. He lives in northern California.